Oliver

FELICITY SNOW

"Maybe the journey isn't about becoming anything. Maybe it's about unbecoming everything that isn't really you, so that you can be who you were meant to be in the first place."
    ~Paulo Coelho

"The best gift you are ever going to give someone: the permission to feel safe in their own skin. To feel worthy. To feel like they are enough."
    ~Hannah Brencher

To everyone who was told that a part of them needed to hide. Don't listen to that shit. Shine so fucking bright you blind someone. The world needs who you were meant to be.

Acknowledgments

To my amazing beta readers, Hawthorne Gray, Donatella Coluzzi, Wren Vale, Sarra Lancey, Angel Corstorphine, and Amanda Martin. Thank you so much for all of your help and support on this story. And to my street team for spreading the word about Oliver and Hunter. I couldn't do this without you!

A special thank you as well to my amazing editors Jen Sharon and Becky Wenzel for making my work shine.

One

OLIVER

"So, son, how's work going?" Father asks, his posh southeast London accent ever present as we sit around the table in my parents' home, eating the pork roast, carrots and potatoes prepared by their housekeeper, Hannah.

It's delicious, and Hannah is such a kind soul, always with a smile to offer whenever I'm here, and a soft kiss to my cheek. She's a stout woman, older, probably late fifties, with dark hair that is graying, a round face and a thick New York accent. She's been working for my parents ever since we moved to New York almost twenty years ago, though sometimes I don't understand how she came to be in their employ, but I guess being paid well is as good a reason to stay as any. While Henry and Isabella Jones are a lot of things, cheap isn't one of them. With the amount of work Hannah does, she deserves to be paid well, plus a rather large bonus for putting up with them, if I'm being honest.

I have the mother of all headaches brewing and I'm completely knackered after a long and very stressful day at work yet again. It's tax season, and that means I'm working even longer hours than normal as an accountant, and dealing with a lot of pissy clients who waited until the last minute to do something that could have been done months ago. For whatever reason, the blame for that falls on me.

Being here is honestly just adding salt to the wound. Family dinners, if you can call them that, as family implies love, encouragement and support, are my least favorite part of every month. The only thing that makes it bearable is having my twin sister, Olivia here with me, and my two year old nephew, Freddie.

"It's exhausting," I sigh.

"Well, nothing in life is easy, son," he responds. "You have to work hard if you want to make something of yourself."

I grit my teeth and rub my fingers over my forehead, closing my eyes as my head begins to pound harder. Why I bother to be honest with this man is beyond me. Never once in his life has he empathized or tried to understand me. His focus has always been on status and wealth, and that's what he expects of his children as well. He treats us more like property than people, the way you would a nice house or a car; things to make him look good; a statement about how well established he is in society. Which is why my sister getting divorced a year ago is something we still don't talk about. Even though she got out of a toxic marriage after six long years, my parents were more horrified that they had "such a scandal" in their family than they were about the fact that she had been mistreated in the first place, telling her she needed to "try harder" to keep her marriage together because, "how will it look, dear?" It took months before Olivia was speaking to them again. She says they apologized, but I have a feeling she came around so that I wouldn't be on my own with them. She's older than me by about eight minutes, and we've always been close; each other's protectors. She and Freddie even lived with me for a few months after the divorce until she could get back on her feet again. I honestly would have loved to have them stay longer, but she said it was important for her to have her own space, and I understood. I was incredibly proud of her for everything she did to make a better life for herself and her son, and very thankful she had friends on her side as well, as my parents were the opposite of helpful.

"How's it going with that girlfriend of yours?" Father asks. "Amy, was it?"

"Amanda," I correct politely. I've mentioned her several times over the past four months that we've been dating, what she does for a living, where she's from, how we met, but the only thing Father cares about is the fact that she's upper class and has a uterus. "It's going fine."

"Marriage on the horizon?" he asks. "You're thirty-six, son. And your mother and I aren't getting any younger. We'll be dead before we have another Jones in the family at this rate. It's your duty to carry on the family name."

"For Christ's sake, Father, we're not the bloody royal family," I retort. "There are other aspirations in life besides children."

"Preposterous," he retorts. "No point in getting married at all if you aren't going to have a family, the way God intended."

"Amanda already has a son, Father, an adult one. I'm not sure more children is what she wants. She's very career minded." I don't bother to tell him that children are not something I want, either, because I am not in the mood for more lecturing.

"Oh, she'll change her mind when she's settled down," Mother pipes up. "Every woman wants a miniature version of her husband." She squeezes father's arm and he pats her hand.

For fuck's sake. Why is it so hard to get them to listen? It's like every goddamn thing I say goes in one ear and out the other.

"Well, you could do worse, I suppose," Father says. "You said she's a lawyer, yes?"

I nod. "And a very good one."

"Well, lots of women put their careers on hold for the sake

of having a family," Mother says. Though I'm not sure what she would know about it since she's never worked a day in her life. And it wasn't like she was much of a mother either, always passing Olivia and I off to nannies so she could go to the next luncheon or social event with her lady friends. I don't begrudge her having a life, but it bothers me that she seems to think she was in any way an involved mother when she was anything but.

"Mother, I just love your bracelet," Olivia chimes in, and I cast her a grateful look. She's come to my rescue on more than one occasion when it seems the only topics of discussion are my single status and their disappointment in my ability to provide them with an heir. It's not about grandchildren, it's about continuing the family line. Never mind the fact that Freddie is sitting right here. To them it's as if he doesn't bloody exist because he is Olivia's son, not mine. It's my job to marry a well to do woman and then convince her to put her career on hold to pop out babies.

"Oh, thank you, dear," Mother preens, showing off the diamond jewelry dangling from her bony wrist. "Your father got it for me as an anniversary gift."

We eat in silence for a moment longer before Mother speaks again.

"Oh, Henry," Mother says, her slender fingers resting on Father's shoulder. "Did you hear about what happened to Agnes and Richard? Such terrible news. They can't show their faces in public, the poor things. After the scandal with their son."

"What's that, dear?" Father asks.

If gossip were an Olympic sport, Isabella Jones would win a gold medal. She's intelligent, though you probably wouldn't know it listening to her speak most of the time, and beautiful, with her long blonde hair up in a bun and wearing a dress that probably costs more than my entire wardrobe. Which is saying something because my suits are not cheap.

Olivia is the spitting image of our mother, with her blonde

hair and green eyes, and her fair complexion, while I in turn, look more like Father. The same auburn hair, blue eyes, and a sharper jawline, fuller lips, and a slightly darker skin tone.

"You know their son, Phillip?" Mother says, "such a shame, because he's such a handsome boy." There's a pause as she shakes her head.

"Go on, dear, don't keep us waiting," Father says. Mother's thin lips purse.

"It's just awful," she says. "Poor Agnes. She's just beside herself. He is a homosexual, darling, and they didn't know it until recently. They caught him in public with another man, and Agnes was mortified. Can you blame her? So awful. She doesn't know what she did wrong. And she's so ashamed and embarrassed."

"The queers will be taking over the country before you know it," Father remarks. "Disgusting is what it is."

My chest tightens and my stomach clenches. I feel a wave of nausea washing over me and reach for my water glass, sweat prickling on my forehead and the back of my neck.

"Sounds to me like the only thing she did wrong was not accept her son for who he is," Olivia retorts, and I almost choke on my drink. Father glances at me, his gaze hard, before turning his attention to my sister as Mother lets out a gasp.

"Olivia, you will not talk to your mother like that. Not in this house." His voice is raised and my cheeks flush as I wipe my face with my napkin.

"I guess it's time for me to leave, then," she states, and scoots out of her chair before turning to unbuckle Freddie from his highchair.

Mother and Father look at my sister with eyes wide in astonishment, and quite frankly so do I, but probably for a different reason. I think getting out of that awful relationship has taught her to speak her mind in a way she never has before, and I can't believe what's happening. Neither of us has ever up and left a family meal, no matter how much we were wanting to. And we've been hearing them spout homophobic bollocks our entire lives.

"I'm going to leave, too," I say.

"Sit down, both of you," Father snarls. "This behavior is absurd!"

My heart is thundering, and there's a very large part of me that is tempted to sit back down as Father demanded, but I don't. I grab my keys and then the nappy bag as Olivia hefts Freddie onto her hip.

"Goodbye Mother, Father," she says. "Tell Hannah thank you for dinner."

"Of all the..." I hear Mother saying as we step out onto the front porch into the cool New York weather. I'm shaking as we walk down the front steps of their Scarsdale mansion.

I open the passenger seat and set the nappy bag inside, before a gentle hand lands on my shoulder. I turn to meet my sister's gaze.

"You alright?" Her eyes flit over my face and I swallow.

"Yeah," I croak out, then clear my throat. "I can't believe we just did that. That you just did that."

Her lips pull into a frown. "They've not had anyone stand up to their bigotry and I am done with it. I'm sorry if I made you uncomfortable."

I shake my head even as I wrap my arms around myself, a shiver running down my spine. "No, it's alright."

"You sure?" she asks, her hand moving to my upper arm. I nod, and she seems skeptical but lets it go.

"You heading home? You look exhausted. I'm sorry work has been so rough."

I give her a small smile as my heart starts to beat at a more normal rhythm and warmth seeps into my bones once again, my adrenaline subsiding. "I'm pretty wired after that. I'll probably drive around for a bit, maybe find a pub. I could use a drink."

"I would join you but I have to get Freddie to bed."

"I know." I kiss her cheek and wave goodbye to Freddie

before she gets in her car and drives off. I'm honestly surprised Father hasn't come out to chastise us and bring us back inside, demanding an apology to Mother, but the door is closed and remains so as I trudge to my Bentley and slide into the driver's seat. I close my eyes and rest my head back, gripping the steering wheel as I take in a deep breath and let it out. Then I start the car and pull out of my parents' driveway.

I honestly don't know where I am going, but my headache resurfaces as I drive, and when I look at the clock on the dash I realize it's been an hour since I left my parents' house.

My phone starts to ring as I pull up to a bar I've never been to. I don't usually frequent this side of town. I ignore the call when I see it's Father, and head inside. Normally I would pick up, because that's what I do. I'm the good son. I cater to my father's every whim. If he says jump I say, "how high?" The only reason I'm dating, period, is because he and Mother were pushing me into a relationship. I thought having a girlfriend would get them to shut up, but all it's done is open the flood gates. Now it's a wedding and grandchildren they want. I could do far worse than Amanda, though. She's lovely, if I'm being honest. Intelligent, kind, hard working. We met in a coffee shop near her office and after sitting together due to lack of room we exchanged numbers and a few days later she called me. Things went from there.

The phone rings again, but for whatever reason, be it the stress or the adrenaline crash, or exhaustion, I'm feeling a bit reckless tonight and don't answer this time either. He can ring all night for all I care.

It's a little after nine pm, so it's not as crowded as it will be in an hour or two, but it's still lively. Music and chatter fill the space around me as I make my way up to the bar and take a seat. I unbutton my suit jacket and slide it off, draping it over the back of the bar stool before rolling up my shirt sleeves. I run my fingers through my hair and let out another heavy sigh. When a sultry voice reaches my ears, I look up to see a young man, probably in his early twenties, with blond hair that falls to just above his shoulders, vivid blue eyes, and a kind smile. He's probably a few inches shorter than my own six feet and is toned and trim, dressed in a snug black T-shirt and jeans that cling to his slender thighs and accentuate his arse, and I let my gaze linger a little longer than is socially acceptable.

Men have always enticed me, but just because I find them attractive, it doesn't mean I'm attracted *to* them. Still though, there's something about the way he moves, oozing confidence, and that toned but slender body that has my heart rate picking up again, and my cock twitching.

I'd wondered since I was thirteen what it might be like to kiss a boy, to have strong arms around me, a firm body pressed up against mine. It didn't mean anything. Just that I appreciated the male form. The sturdiness, the strength, the elegant grace even at times, because some of the most beautiful men I'd ever laid eyes on were slender and more fragile in appearance, but no less captivating. But that was as far as I'd allowed myself to go. Imagining. Never looking for long, never touching. I'd only ever dated women. Though I wasn't particularly attracted to them, I could see objectively that they were attractive and told myself that once I got to know them more, that attraction would grow. That's what I told myself when I fucked Amanda, and that's what I'd been telling myself for years.

The young man takes the towel from over his shoulder and shoves it in his back pocket as he approaches me, and I do my best to ignore my rapidly beating pulse, telling myself he's far too young for me anyway. No thirty-six year old man should be even flirting with the idea of shagging a boy at least fifteen years his junior.

"Hey handsome," he purrs, and my cock jerks. Bloody hell. "What can I get you?"

"Painkiller, please," I say.

"You got it." When my gaze catches on his perky arse

again while he's turned, I tell myself I'm just missing my girlfriend. But I don't look away.

When he turns around and catches my eyes on him I feel my cheeks flushing and clear my throat. He gives me a sultry smile and a wink, making my flush deepen as he makes his way back to me and slides the fruity concoction in front of me, along with a napkin. I take a sip and almost moan as the taste of rum, pineapple juice, orange juice, and coconut cream slides over my taste buds and down my throat.

"Anything else?" he asks, that smile ever present.

"No, thank you," I reply, expecting him to move on to the next customer, but he doesn't.

"I love your accent," he says. "Where are you from?"

I blink. "Scarsdale."

He laughs, and I flush even more.

"Funny and sexy." He's leaning on the bar top now, his face even closer to mine. I can smell the alcohol on him, not his breath, which smells of peppermint, but on his skin and clothes, mixed with an aroma of sweat that I find I do not dislike, and a hint of orange. It's intoxicating and I have to stop myself from leaning closer to breathe him in.

"I hadn't intended to be amusing," I reply instead.

He smiles wider. "You're British, right?"

I nod.

"Damn, you Brits and your sexy af accents are my weakness." He bites his lip as his eyes lower to my mouth. My heart rate spikes again as his gaze lingers for a moment and then returns to my eyes. I see the desire there and I swallow hard. Sweat gathers on the back of my neck and palms as my throat constricts, so much so that when he says, "How'd you come to be in this little neck of the woods?" I have trouble responding and my voice comes out like a goddamn squeak at first, before I clear it and reply.

"I uh…I moved here with my parents and sister when I was fifteen. Well, not here, I suppose, but New York."

"Scarsdale," he says, grinning. I nod. "I used to live near

Scarsdale before I came here for school. My mom is still there."

"Oh, really?"

He nods. "Yeah, I don't go back a lot because of school and work, but it's home. Where in the UK are you from?"

"Southeast London," I say. "Bromley."

His gaze darts to my lips again and his voice is huskier, making a shiver run down my spine when he says, "And are all men from Southeast London as sexy as you?"

My cheeks heat. Shit. I know he's probably only saying these things because it's his job to make the customer happy, and maybe he believes I'll give him a bigger tip if I feel flattered. And fuck, he might be right. "I...I don't know," I say, my gaze locked with his, and then wince internally, as my flush deepens. Christ what is happening to me? I've never been so flustered in my life. *I don't know? Smooth, Oliver.*

"I'm sorry," he says, standing again and pulling the towel out of his back pocket. I see his cheeks pinken slightly too, and wonder if maybe he's not as confident as he appears. "I'm making you uncomfortable. I didn't mean—"

"No!" I'm startled by my own reaction. What the fuck am I doing? I should be accepting his apology and letting him move on, drink my drink and go home. Though I can't imagine driving the hour back to Scarsdale tonight. I'll probably get a hotel. But hotel or not, the last thing I should be doing is engaging with him. Is it so wrong though? It's just a bit of fun. And I can't stop. He's intriguing, and I find myself unwinding as he smiles at me once more, my stress beginning to evaporate, my shoulders relaxing the tiniest bit. Some of that is the drink, I'm sure, but some of it is him.

He grins, his shoulders relaxing as well, and I find myself wanting to lick the dimple that appears on his right cheek. "So what brings you to a bar an hour from home?"

I sigh again. "It's been a rather long day, I'm afraid. Just needed a drive, and a drink, and ended up here, I suppose."

"Work stress?" he asks, and I give a small smile. His

features turn down slightly like he's actually genuinely interested in my life, and wants to help. Like he cares.

"Among other things," I say, before taking another sip of my drink.

"You know," he says, his voice lowering as he leans over the counter again, this time even closer. He seems a bit flustered but I can't understand why. He bites that bottom lip again as his eyes meet mine, and I feel my cock twitching once more. Fucking hell. "I know of a great way to unwind."

My eyes widen and I choke on the last bit of drink sliding down my throat, causing me to gasp. I bring my napkin to my mouth as my face flames, my eyes watering slightly. "I beg your pardon," I say, a hand on my chest. He flushes beautifully, his smile widening as he glances down. My eyes dart around the room before returning to him. I lower my voice. "Are you asking what I think you are?"

"No pressure," he says, like he just asked if I wanted to watch a ball game or play golf on the weekend, not fuck him in the loo. "It doesn't have to be sex, sex. I could blow you. But the other thing is definitely on the table, too."

I find myself staring at those plump pillowy lips and my cock jumps at the thought of having them around me, swallowing me, those stunning blue eyes locked with mine. I'm sporting a semi in seconds, and my brain is screaming at me to say no! Why the fuck haven't I said no? Said I have a girlfriend, that I'm not fucking gay, that I have never been with a man before, that he's too damn young for me? So many reasons for me to be shaking my head right now.

But I don't.

"I'm very good," he says, his voice seductive in a way that makes me shiver.

"I'm sure you are," I reply before I can stop myself, and he chuckles, making my cheeks flame for the millionth time in the last twenty minutes.

"Well," he says, "I'm gonna go serve my other customers. You let me know if there's anything I can do for you." He leans closer and beckons with his finger for me to do the same. I find myself not even hesitating, and we're so close that his mouth is right next to my ear when he says, "And I do mean anything, gorgeous." Then he stands and winks at me, before walking away.

Bloody hell.

HUNTER

Damn, what is it about that guy?

I have to try really hard not to look back at the sexy British man as I serve the other guests at the counter. I've never been so instantly captivated by someone, but one look at him and I was a goner. Then he opened that sexy as fuck mouth and I thought my legs might give out. Damn, as if his body wasn't gorgeous enough with those auburn waves, cobalt eyes and the freckles dusted across his nose and cheeks, he has to have the sexiest voice in the goddamn universe. I've always been a sucker for British accents and his is fucking perfection.

He didn't quite seem to know what to do with me, did he? I smile at the thought as I remember him choking on his drink and his eyes widening so far I thought they might pop out of his head when I propositioned him. Fuck, he's fun to flirt with. The way his cheeks flush and he stumbles over his words, it's addicting.

I can feel his eyes on me as I move around, and turn to give him a quick wink before returning to my work. I grin when I see that flush creeping up his lightly stubbled cheeks again, as he runs his fingers through those thick waves. God, I want to get my hands in that hair, grip it, tug it, slide my fingers through it and feel how fucking soft it must be. I can tell by looking at him he has money. The suit and watch alone must cost more than my fucking car. That's not saying a whole lot cause my car is a piece of junk, but, if that's the case, I know whatever he wears in his hair is just as extravagant. Damn, he smells incredible too. Like vanilla and gingerbread.

I want him more than I think I've wanted anyone, but I won't mention hooking up again. I'm tempted to, but I'm not pushy, and he knows I'm available if he decides he wants me, too. Consent is important to me in anyone I fuck.

Chances are he won't be back any time soon, or at all if he lives an hour away. This is probably my only chance to know what those full lips would feel like against mine. What it would be like to hold his cheeks in my hands and feel his stubble under my palms.

Why does the thought of never seeing him again make my chest ache when I don't even know him and all he is is a potential hook up?

I don't date. Life is too crazy for that right now, but being in my junior year of college and having the course load that I do, on top of this job, I need a way to unwind sometimes. Normally I don't have any trouble finding someone to fuck, and I'm pretty sure I could take home just about any guy here. Well, any not-straight guy. It's not a gay bar, but it pays well and I enjoy it enough.

The thing is though, I don't want just any guy. I want him. In all of his awkward adorableness. He's got to be at least ten years older than my twenty-one years, but I've always liked more mature men.

"Hey, we're running low on chips," my coworker Jordan tells me, as he mixes a customer's drink.

"Already?"

He shrugs.

"I got it," I say and head back to the storeroom that's around the corner and down the hall. I've just grabbed the chips when I hear the door opening and closing. I don't turn to see who it is right away. "Dude, I said I had it."

When there's no reply I turn my head, and don't even have a chance to speak again before soft, warm hands are gripping my face and full, wet lips press to mine.

I grunt, then groan before I grip the other man's hair, pulling him back. His face is flushed, his freckles standing out even more against his ivory skin, and his pupils are blown wide as his chest rises and falls. Fuck.

"You're not allowed back here," I tell him, my voice husky.

"Shall I leave, then?" His breaths are coming heavier, and my cock jerks at how sexy his voice sounds when he's turned on.

"Fuck, no," I growl, the chips falling to the floor as I grip his face in my palm, my other hand still holding tightly to his silky hair, and press my lips to his. He moans and the sound goes straight to my cock. I'm hard in an instant as his lips move against mine. I kiss him harder, wanting to hear more of those sexy as fuck noises, and he doesn't disappoint. He's so fucking eager it's turning me on even more.

Fuck.

I spin him around and press him up against the wall, still gripping his hair. He grunts and I feel his cock thickening against my thigh as I continue to kiss him. God, he feels huge, and my own cock jerks again, my mouth watering at the thought of having his dick in my mouth.

I slide my leg between his and he moans when his cock comes in contact with my thigh. My tongue slides along his lower lip and he opens for me, making my cock throb at the taste of pineapple, orange juice, and coconut filling my mouth.

"Fuck, you're delicious," I say, pulling away. His hair is a mess from having my fingers in it and his lips are spit slicked and swollen from my kisses. His blue eyes are so dark they look almost black in the dim light of the storeroom. Sweat is beaded on his forehead and neck and it's the fucking hottest thing I've ever seen.

I lick along his lip, then slide my tongue in his mouth again and shift slightly as I grip his wrists, pinning them above his head as our cocks align. He groans into my mouth and ruts against me, and fucking hell, I love it. Love that he is so desperate and is letting me take control.

"Damn, London, you're going to be the death of me," I murmur into his ear as we both thrust our hips, the friction of our cocks through our pants fucking delicious. I kiss his jaw right below his ear and he shudders. I make my way down to his chin, pressing kisses, and he tilts his neck back on a moan, granting me access. He gasps, and jerks his hips against me as I lick a stripe up his neck, pausing momentarily to nibble on his Adam's apple, before sliding my tongue up his chin and capturing his lips with mine again, both of us moaning into the kiss.

"Nnnnggg," he whimpers, and God, I'm so damn hard, my cock is leaking like crazy. I devour his mouth for several more moments before pulling away. If we keep at this I'm going to come in my pants. Especially if he keeps making those noises.

Releasing his wrists, I sink slowly to my knees, and his eyes darken even more, his chest rising and falling as he watches me. His cock twitches in his dress pants and it's enough to make me fucking moan as I lean in and press kisses to it through the fabric. God, he's hot as hell, standing above me, hair a rumpled mess, pupils blown wide and the sleeves on his dress shirt rolled up to his elbows, his tie askew.

"Fuck," he gasps as I alternate between kissing and nibbling on his cock, my own cock throbbing in my jeans. His precum is leaking out through his slacks, he's so turned on. I wonder if he could come just from this. Something tells me he could, and fuck, that's enough to make even more precum leak from my slit and down my aching shaft. But I want that giant cock in my mouth. I want to know what he tastes like. I need to know.

I grip his belt and start to unbuckle it as I press kiss after kiss to his tip and feel it twitching against me again and again, hearing his pants, and groans of pleasure as he grips my hair.

"Fuck," he breathes. "I'm going to come if you don't stop."

I look him in the eyes and lick the precum from his pants, and he shudders, his legs shaking as he lets out a noise somewhere between a growl and a whimper.

Then his belt is open and I'm pulling his pants down. There's a clank as they hit the floor around his ankles, and I stare at his erection through his boxer briefs. My mouth waters and I look up at him again. His fingers are still gripping my hair and I fucking love it.

"Can I?" I ask.

"Fuck, yes," he says, and it sounds more like a plea than anything else. I grip his waistband and pull the underwear down, his cock springing free and almost slapping me in the face. Fucking hell, he's huge. I'm salivating as I look at him. He's uncut, and must be close to eight inches in length with an impressive girth as well. His cock oozes precum as I stare at it, the head red and angry, a prominent vein running up the center. His balls are just as enticing, hanging low and heavy between his splayed thighs, and his pubic hair is wild. I have a feeling he doesn't manscape, and I am completely fine with that.

I lean in and lick the tip, moaning as his precum lands on my tongue, his taste exploding in my mouth. God, that's good. I want more. So much more. I open wide and take in just the head and his grip tightens in my hair, making me moan around him. He twitches in my mouth and I take him deeper, blissed out by the weight of him on my tongue.

"Fuck," he curses. "That's good." I have a feeling he's holding back, trying not to be to rough, but I love having my face fucked and his cock is the most incredible thing I've ever had in my mouth. He can do whatever the fuck he wants to me. I grip his shaft with one hand and stroke him as I suck and lick, my other hand gripping his thigh, and he trembles.

"Bloody hell," he gasps, then groans, his head hitting the wall as I swallow him deeper.

I pop off of him and he immediately looks at me. God, he's a vision. "Don't hold back," I tell him. "I like it rough. I want you to use me. Come in my mouth, gorgeous. Let me taste you." His eyes heat and he nods, before I'm taking him down my throat again and he does exactly as I instructed. His hips thrust and his cock slides in and out of my mouth relentlessly, making my eyes water and saliva slide down his shaft and along my chin, dripping onto the floor between us. I move my hand from his cock and use it to unbutton my pants and take out my own cock. It's so hard it hurts, and I almost sob when I have it in my hand. I begin to stroke myself as he uses me.

"Fuck." He grips my hair in both hands now and thrusts again and again. "Christ," I hear and then his cock pulses in my mouth, and he's spilling down my throat. The taste of him is enough to make my own orgasm barrel into me and I moan around his dick, still in my mouth as my own release fills my hand and drips onto the floor. My throat feels wrecked, but it was absolutely worth it.

He slides out of me and a moment later he's kneeling in front of me with a towel he must have grabbed from nearby, wiping the tears, spit and snot from my face.

Fuck. He's cleaning me off, and it's so tender and caring I find myself blushing.

"That was incredible," he says, then kisses me. I kiss him back before bringing my hand up for him to clean off as well. When he grips my wrist in his hand and brings my cum covered one to his mouth, before his tongue slides out and licks up my release, letting out a moan as he swallows, I fucking shiver.

"Damn," I say. "You're full of surprises, aren't you, London?" He flushes and grins, making my heart skip a beat. I hadn't seen him smile until now. It's sexy as fuck.

We help each other stand and he slides his underwear and pants back up as I tuck myself back into my jeans. Then I find the bag of chips that Jordan has been waiting on for God knows how long now.

Shit.

"I have to go," I say hurriedly, even though everything in me wants to stay and kiss those perfect lips until I can't anymore, either from exhaustion or from my jaw being so sore I have to stop or risk permanent injury.

Fuck, my heart is racing. I press my lips to his once more and have to force myself to pull away. "Stay," I beg him. "I get off in two hours. Come home with me."

His eyes widen.

I dart out of the room before he can answer.

Two

OLIVER

Jesus Christ, I don't know what's come over me. I've never done anything so reckless in my life, but I couldn't stop myself. I couldn't leave without knowing what he tasted like. Peppermint and a hint of cherries. It was delicious. Everything about him is delicious. He gave me the best blow job, and I came harder than I ever have before.

The way he gripped me, kissed me, looked at me. I want more. I've never felt more wanted, owned, or worshiped in my life. I'm shaking a little with the knowledge that I just cheated on my girlfriend of four months. And the worst part is, even though it makes me a complete and utter bellend, I want to do it again. With him. Fuck, I don't even know his name but I can't go back to Scarsdale without knowing what it's like to feel him inside me, surrounding me.

I was stunned when he asked me to stay, but I am staying. Even though I'm exhausted and even though I have three missed calls from Amanda on my phone and just as many texts, I ignore them, as I watch the handsome young stranger moving around behind the bar, filling orders, mixing drinks, and chatting with customers, every once in a while flashing me a dazzling smile or a wink, making my cheeks heat every damn time.

Even though he's significantly younger than me, there's something about how he talked to me, how he swallowed me down and told me to use him, let me fuck his face with no mercy, that I can't get out of my mind. It was perfect. He was perfect.

Over the next two hours he doesn't find much time to visit with me, but maybe that makes the prospect of fucking back at his place even more enticing. The waiting, the anticipation. I do order a couple more drinks, but stick to non alcoholic beverages. I don't want to be drunk when we leave. If I'm going to have my first time with a man, I want to be completely alert and aware.

"Hey," he says, coming over to me with a grin on his face. "You stayed. Does that mean you'll come home with me?"

I nod.

His smile grows wider, and I can't help smiling back. "Give it a couple of minutes and then come find me in the parking lot."

I nod again. When he emerges from behind the bar and heads around the corner I wait the allotted amount of time and then leave some cash on the bar before grabbing my suit jacket off the back of the chair and heading towards the door.

I spot him in the car park, standing next to an older, gray Hyundai Elantra, the paint peeling off the bumper, and the passenger side mirror missing, his smile just as wide as before. He's wearing a striking leather jacket over his work clothes now and it makes him look a little bit older, and a hell of lot sexier.

"Ready?" he says. "I know it's nothing fancy, but it works." He gestures to the car. "Wanna follow me?" He turns around and opens the driver's side door. I should be telling someone what I'm doing, right? But I can't. Who do I tell that

I'm going to a relative stranger's house to fuck when I'm in a relationship? God, I'm being stupid. I've never been so impulsive and careless, but tonight seems to be my night for it.

I nod and take my keys from my pocket, pressing the keyfob and making the lights flash. "Of course you have a Bentley," he says, but there's no disdain in his voice, and I think I even detect a small smile. I flush. "See you there?"

I nod, then head towards my car as he climbs into his. He waits until he knows I'm able to follow and pulls out of the car park.

Christ, what the fuck am I doing?

HUNTER

Ten minutes later, I'm pulling into the parking lot of my apartment complex, and a second after that, London pulls up beside me in his Bentley.

I climb out of my car and he follows, looking around. He seems a bit unsure and I don't really blame him. I have a feeling this isn't the kind of area he is accustomed to. It's not bad, but it's not upscale either. I notice that his suit jacket is still missing, and he's removed his tie, the top couple of buttons on his dress shirt undone, giving me a peak at his ivory chest and the dusting of auburn hair scattered across it. My cock jerks at the idea of burying my face in that hair and inhaling his scent.

"You alright?" I ask. "I know it's not Scarsdale, but it's safe."

He nods and then follows me inside and up the stairs to the third floor.

"Is there not a bloody lift in this place?" he asks, his breaths coming heavier as we reach the third floor hallway.

I chuckle. "You tired, old man? I knew you were older than me, but I didn't think you were that old."

He narrows his eyes at me in a way that is more endearing

than anything else and I laugh again. "Sod off," he replies, and I laugh more.

"My roommates are out," I tell him, stopping in front of the apartment I share with two other guys. "So you can be as loud as you want." I wink and he flushes bright pink.

"You enjoy flustering me, don't you?" he says.

"Maybe," I admit. Then glance down at his lips. My cock jerks again and suddenly I am a lot more eager to get inside than I was thirty seconds ago. I turn the key in the lock and and as soon as I hear it click I push the door open, grabbing his arm and pulling him in after me.

"Fuck," he curses as he trips slightly, and I laugh as I close the door and lock it. Then I'm gripping him and shoving him so his back is against it.

"Sorry, handsome," I purr, then take his mouth with mine again. I kiss him hungrily, my tongue sliding inside that warm, wet heat and making me groan before I pull back. "You do things to me."

"Likewise," he murmurs, his pupils dilated and his voice that deep rumble that tells me he's as horny as I am. I feel his dick twitching against my thigh.

"Mmmmm," I groan, as I reach down to stroke him through his pants. He hisses and pulls my face to his again, pressing his lips against mine as he thrusts into my hand. Fuck, that's hot.

"Bedroom," I say, pulling away. I slide my shoes off, leaving them by the door. He does the same, before I am taking his hand and pulling him down the hall towards my room. I don't bother turning any lights on on the way. I don't give a fuck, and the only thing I want right now is to have him underneath me. I flip the light switch once we get to my room and the lamp on the bedside table turns on, casting a warm glow over the space. It's perfect.

Gripping his face in my palms, I kiss him feverishly for several seconds before pulling away. "Strip," I tell him, and he listens, sliding out of his dress pants and shirt as I slip my jacket off and toss it aside, then pull my T-shirt over my head and undo my jeans.

Seconds later we're both standing there naked and my cock jerks at the sight of him, precum oozing out and sliding down my shaft. "God, you're sexy," I say, and he bites his lip. It's the most adorable thing ever. His cock is deliciously hard and his own precum leaks out, making my mouth water once again at the memory of what he tastes like. Now that he's got his shirt off I have a perfect view of the smattering of auburn chest hair across his pecs and abdomen, and as I move closer I see the dusting of freckles along his shoulders and arms.

"Fuck, London, you make me so damn hard," I growl as I grip his hair and tilt his head slightly, slotting my lips against his again. He moans in my mouth as our cocks press together when I shove him against the door once more. I take both of us in my hand and start to stroke us together, using our precum as lube. He's so big I can barely get my hand around both of us. He moans and whimpers into my mouth as I work both of our shafts, the feeling of his naked cock against mine utterly sinful, and I kiss him harder, my tongue sliding even further into his mouth. I suck and lick, and he grips my hair in turn, kissing me back just as fiercely.

"Hmmm, nggg," he whines and I pull back. "Stop, please," he pants. "I don't want to come yet."

I grin and release him, but continue to stroke myself as he watches, his eyes darkening as he licks his lips. "You want this, beautiful?" He nods. "On the bed, then," I order, and he moves instantly. God, it turns me on to have him obeying me. I've always loved being in charge in bed. It's not a requirement but I certainly prefer it.

"How do you want me?" he asks, stopping by the side of the bed and looking back at me. His cock is straining, slick with our precum and it glistens in the low light of the room, making my own cock twitch at the sight. He seems slightly hesitant, and I don't know why.

"You sure about this?" I ask, and he nods, so I say, "any way you want is fine with me, beautiful."

He climbs onto the bed on his hands and knees. "How's this?" he asks.

I lick my lips as I move closer. God, that's a gorgeous ass. Round and full, and begging to be filled, to be used. "Good," I say, then climb on behind him and press kisses to his spine, making him shiver. "You seem a little nervous, handsome. You sure you're okay?"

He nods. "Yes, I…just, go slow. And be gentle."

My lips leave his naked skin and I ask, "You ever bottomed before?" He shakes his head. "You're in for a treat, then, sweetheart. And don't worry, I'll take good care of you. You're safe with me."

He nods, and I continue to press kisses down the length of his spine until I reach his perky ass cheeks and begin to nibble and lick on the taught globes. He gasps and I hear his breath picking up as I grip his hips and suck on his ass cheeks.

"Fuck," he cries, and my cock jerks, precum leaking onto the sheets below me.

"Mmm, you taste good, London," I purr, before spreading his cheeks and blowing on his hole. He jerks and swears again and I grin. "You like that?"

He nods and I grin wider. I blow on his hole one more time, making him spasm, before I say, "Lower your top half onto the mattress, gorgeous." He does and I groan as his gorgeous pucker flutters, practically asking me to suck and lick on it, to fuck it. Fuck, yes. I lean in and lick a stripe from his taint up to his hole, and he bucks.

"Christ," he almost shouts, and it's a really good thing my roommates are out.

I chuckle, then grip his hips tighter and repeat the action a few more times, making him squirm and let out a series of curses, before I slide my tongue into his hole.

"Fuck," he cries, and I have to grip him tighter to keep him from moving away as I tongue fuck him. God he's delicious. His sounds have my cock throbbing and I feel him shaking as he mewls.

"Shit, I can't," he whimpers. "Please." I slide my tongue out of him and wipe the saliva off my chin. His body is quaking and it's the hottest thing I've ever seen. "Fuck, I almost came," he groans, catching his breath.

"Would that be so bad?" I tease, and he looks back at me over his shoulder.

"I want to come with you inside me," he says, and God, yes, I want that too. Want to feel his hole clenching around me, choking my cock while he releases.

I press a few more kisses to his lower back and ass before I say, "Roll over. I want to see you when I fuck you." His cheeks pinken, but he does as I ask, and God, the sight of him staring up at me, face flushed, sweat beaded on his chest and forehead, hair a mess makes me groan. I grip his knees and shove them apart a bit more, then slide between them and hover over him. I've never fucked any of my other hook ups this way. I always took them from behind because it was less intimate, and that's how I wanted it. Just a transaction. But I can't help but feel like whatever this is, it's more. I lower my lips to his and kiss him again. He's staring at me when I pull away. "Fuck, you're beautiful," I whisper. I feel his cock jerk against my stomach as his face flushes again, and I moan. He likes that. He likes to be complimented. To be told he's beauti-ful, good, sexy.

I kiss him again, deeper this time, and he moans into my mouth. I feel his legs spreading wider and lifting, his knees brushing against my arms. "You want my cock, gorgeous?" I ask, pulling away.

"Please," he says. I kiss him and then sit back.

"Lift your hips," I instruct. He does, and I grab the pillow next to him and shove it under his ass, elevating him slightly. "Now, spread those pretty legs for me again, baby," I say. His cock jerks again as more precum leaks out.

"That's it," I praise, when I see that pretty pucker once

again, fluttering eagerly. I grab the lube from the nightstand and slick my fingers up, then I slide closer and tap my finger at his entrance, making him gasp. "That feel good?" I say. He nods, but doesn't speak.

"Talk to me, beautiful. Use your words, or you don't get my cock."

"Yes," he breathes. "Fuck, yes, it feels good. Please, don't stop."

I grin and press against his hole a second time, then circle the gorgeous pucker a few times, before sliding my middle finger inside him. He lets out the most incredible moan and throws his head back, his neck muscles strained as his ass clenches around my finger, his thighs spasming.

"Fuck," he cries, as I move inside him. "Fuck, that's good."

I chuckle. "You haven't seen anything yet, handsome." I slide out and he fucking whimpers, his head lifting as he stares at me. I slick my fingers up again and then slide back inside him, two this time. His hips buck as he cries out.

"Shit!" He's breathing heavier now and more sweat breaks out across his upper body.

"Open your eyes," I tell him. "I want to look at you while I finger fuck this pretty little hole."

He stares at me, and nods. I scissor my fingers and he mewls. "It burns a little."

"Should I stop?" I ask, my fingers stalling inside him. He shakes his head vehemently.

"No, fuck, God, no, don't stop," he practically whines. "Please don't stop."

I scissor my fingers a few more times before I search for that soft rubbery spot inside him. When I reach it and nudge my finger against it, his entire body jolts as he curses again, and reaches down to grip his cock. He squeezes, no doubt to keep himself from coming.

"Shit," he says again and I see his eyes watering.

"No coming until I'm inside you, London," I say. "You got

that? I want this pretty hole spasming around my cock when you unload." He swallows and nods, and I add a third finger, stretching him even more.

"Shit, please," he begs after only a few seconds. "I can't. I need you inside me." It's not lost on me that neither of us have shared our names. I thought about it, but I know I have to let him go after we're finished and knowing his name will make that even harder. I don't know his reason, but I don't care. Though hearing my name on his lips as he moans, and begs, and whimpers, or even better, when he comes, would be heaven.

If he's willing, though, maybe I'll get his number before he leaves, hopefully not until morning. He is from Scarsdale so I could see him when I go back home. Hell, I'd make a trip just to see him, and not just for sex.

He's stretched enough now, so I nod and slide my fingers out before grabbing a condom and more lube. I slide on the condom and slick myself up. "Put your legs over my arms," I tell him. He complies and his hands grip my shoulders as my cock presses against his entrance, making us both moan.

"Oh, fuck." My cock pushes past his tight ring and slips inside. Fuck, I'm not even close to all the way inside him, but it feels so damn good. I close my eyes and let out a deep breath. Then grip his hand and pull it to my lips, pressing kisses to it. "You okay?" I ask.

He nods. "It hurts."

"It will hurt some, just for a little bit, but I'll go slow, I promise. It'll be worth it. Trust me?" He nods again and my heart soars. I kiss his fingers a few more times and then release his hand and grip his hair instead. "Kiss me," I say, and he lifts his head to capture my lips with his as I continue to slide inside him, inch by inch. I do as I said I would, going as slowly as I can, and he stretches to accept me, his tight heat like a vice around my cock.

"Fuck," he groans, pulling away from the kiss. "It feels like you're splitting me in two." He lets out a breath and I smile as I slide a little bit further in, moving my hand down to rub circles on his abdomen, feeling his treasure trail under my fingers and purring at the sensation.

"Your ass is taking my cock so well, baby," I tell him, and his cock jerks between us. Fuck, he's a slut for praise. I let out another breath as I bottom out, my balls resting against his ass. His chest is rising and falling as he grips my shoulders so tightly I'm pretty sure he'll leave bruises, and I press my forehead to his. "So fucking perfect," I murmur against his lips.

"I'm gonna fuck you so good, sweetheart." I don't know where all the terms of endearment are coming from but I can't help it. It's like he's pulling them out of me and I don't have any control over the shit coming out of my mouth.

I slide out almost all the way and then back in, and his thighs tremble. I do it one more time, and he whimpers. "Don't hold back," I tell him when he bites his lip. "I want to hear you, gorgeous. I want to know what I do to you."

"Fuck!" he cries as I slide out one more time and then thrust back in harder. God, he feels incredible. I know I'm not going to last long.

"Legs over my shoulders, baby," I instruct, and he obeys without hesitation, his eyes lidded, and his hair dampened with sweat. I moan at the sight of his perfect hole swallowing my cock as I slide out and back in again, his body practically bent in half as I impale him on my cock.

"Oh, God," he whimpers. "Oh, Christ, Oh, fuck, fuck." I thrust my hips and the new angle has my cock pegging his prostate over and over as he mewls underneath me.

"Fuck, London, you feel so good," I growl, gripping his hair. I thrust a few more times. "Your hole is so greedy for me, isn't it?"

His cock jerks at the same time his hole spasms around me, and I groan. "Look at me," I demand, and his eyes lock with mine. "I want you looking into my eyes when I make you come, beautiful. You're gonna remember who made you feel this way." He groans as my cock hits his sweet spot again and again. "God, you're so damn perfect, aren't you?"

His hands grip my shoulder so hard I feel his nails digging in, and then he's throwing his head back on a growl as he sprays his release between us and his hole spasms around me. "Fuck," I groan, picking up my pace and slamming into him again. It only takes three more thrusts before my load is shooting inside of him and filling the condom. Then I'm kissing him, and my chest aches at the thought of never doing this again. What is it about him that has me so enraptured?

He was so damn perfect.

I pull out slowly, then lean over and lap his release from his stomach, making him gasp and jerk slightly.

"Fuck," he says, his stomach sinking in as he grabs my hair to keep it from falling into his cum. I hum around the taste of him as it slides down my throat, then press a kiss to the tip of his cock. It twitches, and I kiss it again, before sliding my finger through his release that's on my stomach and lifting it to my mouth, sucking it inside and swallowing again. Then I'm moving up and pressing my mouth to his.

He opens for me and I slide my tongue inside, letting him taste himself on me. After a final peck to his lush lips I remove the condom and tie it off before tossing it in the trash can beside the bed, and collapsing next to him.

"You okay?" I ask, running my finger over his pecs, feeling the soft hairs there.

"Very much," he replies. He looks exhausted but sated. He reaches over to stroke my cheek. "I should go."

My eyes meet his. "Please don't." I can't stand the thought of him leaving right now. I've never wanted a hook up to stay a second after we've both gotten off, but for some reason it's different with him.

He swallows, his fingers drifting to the ends of my hair as he plays with the strands. "I have a long drive home."

"Make it in the morning," I urge. "Just one night here,

with me. Please? You can shower and I'll wash your clothes, feed you breakfast. Besides, you're exhausted and it's late. You really shouldn't be driving."

His gaze flits over my face and his eyes are filled with uncertainty, but he nods. "Very well." I chuckle and kiss him. Then curl up by his side and drift to sleep.

Three

OLIVER

I wake several hours later to the sun shining through the bedroom curtain and blink, then jolt when I feel a warm, very naked body against mine and hard cock pressing against my arse. Memories from the previous night flood my mind and I slide out of my companion's embrace as carefully as I can so as not to wake him. In the light of day, the realization of what I have done crashes into me and I start to panic. It's not just the fact that I slept with another person when I have a girl-friend waiting for me in Scarsdale that terrifies me. It's the fact that that other person was a man.

So why did I do it? I wish I could blame it on the alcohol, but I can't. The truth is, I did it because I wanted to. And maybe because if sleeping with a man didn't turn out to be everything I'd ever imagined it to be, I could move on. Move on from these ideas and dreams of finding another man to share my life with. Marry Amanda and forget that I ever wanted something different.

But that backfired so horrifically because it wasn't terrible at all. It was incredible. It was everything.

Christ, I can't stay here. I have to get home and cleaned up and changed before I start work. Before I see Amanda again.

Christ, Amanda. I dig through the pile of clothes on the floor and find my phone in my trouser pocket, pulling it out. Looking at the screen, I have twelve missed texts and calls from her and another six from my father. I groan quietly and run a hand through my hair.

Fuck. What have I done? I've always considered myself a decent man. I've never cheated on any of my previous girlfriends. Not that there were many. I certainly didn't enter that bar last night with the intention of cheating, but I did.

I look back at the sleeping man who fucked me so good I can still feel his cock inside me. My body shudders remembering the words he spoke, how he praised me. I'd never had someone talk to me like that before and I loved it, more than I care to admit. Loved the feeling of being filled, of submitting. It was freeing, to let go.

I know I told him I would stay and shower, and have breakfast with him, but one look at him rumpled and dozing under the sheets and I know I can't. I've already fucked up so much in the last twenty-four hours, I can't do it again.

So what if it was the best sex I've ever had. It was just an experiment. Nothing more. A way to relieve stress.

So why is it so hard to leave, knowing I will probably never see him again? Shouldn't see him again. I ache to touch him, to run my fingers through his golden hair, to see those beautiful blue eyes looking back at me, that smile on his handsome face.

But I don't touch him. I don't speak. I stand and pull my briefs on, then my trousers. Telling myself I am doing the right thing, even though it feels very much like leaving him is the biggest mistake of my life.

God, my clothes reek of sex. I have to get home and cleaned up before someone sees me. I should never have been here. I can't be here.

I'm shaking as I button my shirt and tuck it in, then buckle my belt. I grab my phone and even though I want to leave my number and a note, telling him where he can find me or asking him if he wants to do this again, because I would gladly drive an hour to be with him a second time, I don't do that either. I slip out of the room and close the door behind me. The apartment is silent as I make my way towards the front door. I slide my shoes on, make sure I have my keys and wallet, and then make my way out of the building, my chest aching the entire three flights of stairs down to my car.

When I get inside I close the door, and hands shaking, I pick up my phone, then take a deep breath and press call. Amanda's sunny voice greets me on the other end and I have to rub my chest as the ache inside deepens.

"Oliver?" she says. "Oh my God, are you okay? I called you a dozen times and texted you and you didn't answer. I was getting worried."

"I'm alright, love," I tell her. "Just tired. I had a long day at work yesterday and went to bed early."

"You sound a little funny," she says, and I chuckle. It's not humorous, at all, really, the situation, but I don't know what else to do. It's either that or scream.

"I'm okay," I say again. "Listen, would you want to get dinner tonight? Someplace special?"

"Ooh, I would love that. Are you sure you're up for it?"

"Absolutely," I lie. "Pick you up at eight?"

"Okay," she says, a smile evident in her voice. I hang up and feel tears sliding down my cheeks as I pull out of the lot.

I pull myself together before I ring Father.

"It's about time," he snarls. "Where do you and your sister get off, treating your mother like that? We raised you to respect your elders, and I will not tolerate—"

"Father, I've decided to ask Amanda to marry me," I interrupt.

There's silence for a beat before he replies. "Well, I see you took to heart what your mother and I said last night. Glad to hear it. You'll be bringing her around for dinner soon, then, I

take it. I'll have your mother tell Hannah to prepare something special for the occasion."

"That would be nice, Father, thank you."

"In light of the good news I suppose we can put last
night's behavior behind us. You really ought to have a talk
with your sister, though, Oliver. I fear she's becoming too
autonomous, now that she is on her own, with no man to
guide her."

"Of course, Father."

"We'll see you and Amanda in a month, then."

"Yes, Father." I hang up my phone and wipe more tears
from my cheeks.

It's shortly after I arrive back at my apartment that my phone
rings again. I answer when I see it's my sister calling.

"Hello?"

"Hey, Oliver, I hear congratulations are in order." Her tone
is more reserved than congratulatory, though.

"Christ, has Mother been spreading the word already? I
only just told Father an hour ago. And I haven't even popped
the bloody question yet."

"But you're planning to, soon?" she asks.

"Very soon, in fact," I tell her, shutting the door behind me
and setting my keys on the hook inside, before toeing off my
dress shoes. Why does the thought of washing these clothes
make my chest ache? My trousers have precum on them that
leaked through when that beautiful boy was touching me,
kissing me, kissing my cock through them, and it made me so
unbelievably hard I thought I might come before he'd even
gotten them off. Everything I'm wearing smells of his apartment, his room. I don't even want to shower because this is a
scent I want to remember for the rest of my life. Christ, that
sounds insane, but it's true.

"And this is what you really want?" she says.

"Why wouldn't it be?" I reply.

"No reason. I just want you to be happy, Oliver. If Amanda makes you happy, then I'm happy for you."

"Thank you, I appreciate that. Though I'm not even certain she'll say yes."

"I guess you'll find out."

I manage a small smile. "I guess I will."

HUNTER

Three months later

"Hey, you heading out soon?"

I turn to see my friend and roommate, Matt standing outside my door, his hand on the frame. He's tall. Taller than me, with curly brown hair and deep brown eyes.

"Yeah." I turn back to my empty suitcase and sigh, and a minute later jump when I hear his voice next to mine.

"You do realize that in order to pack, you actually have to put things in your suitcase."

I narrow my eyes at him. "You can go back where you came from," I reply, and he laughs.

"Seriously, dude, you've been in a funk for weeks. Months. Going home, getting a change of scenery, taking that trip, it'll be good for you. You and your mom get along well enough, don't you?"

I nod. We're relatively close, since we've only ever had each other, and she's always been accepting of me being gay. She had me when she was only eighteen and worked her butt off, even with a toddler, to put herself through college and law school. She's been a lawyer in Scarsdale for twelve years. She's kind of a badass, actually.

She got engaged to her boyfriend almost three months ago now and she wants me to come home and meet him before the wedding. They have a road trip planned that I'm supposed to join them on so we can bond before the big day.

I'm not opposed to it necessarily, I just think it seems a little fast.

"Yeah, we do," I say, "I'm just feeling kinda weird about everything. Don't you think it's a bit soon to get engaged when you've only dated for four months? And the wedding is in two months. Isn't that fast?"

Matt shrugs. "Beats the hell out of me. My parents were engaged after six months. I don't think there's a timeline for these things. Just whatever works for the couple."

I sigh. "Maybe you're right," I admit. I've been stuck in my head ever since I woke up to find that the sexy British man from the bar had left without saying goodbye, or even leaving a note, or his number. He was just gone. I told myself it wasn't a big deal. It was just sex, but that didn't explain how I'd found myself lying in bed with tears sliding down my cheeks at the realization that I would never see him again, and that apparently, he had no desire to see me again.

Fuck, my eyes are tearing up at the memory and I wipe at them quickly before Matt can see. It's been three fucking months and I still can't get him out of my head.

"Hey," he says, placing his hand on my shoulder, "that guy was a douche, okay? He doesn't deserve you."

"Yeah," I say. So why can't I move on from him? Why is he in my every waking thought? Why have I had to convince myself that driving to Scarsdale to search for him isn't a good idea? I'll be close enough now that I'm going back home, but what are the chances of me running into him there? It's not a huge town but it's not a tiny one, either. And I have no idea where to start looking, or what I'd even say if I found him. I'd look so pathetic. He let me fuck him once, for Christ's sake, and he doesn't owe me anything.

I've never been so hung up on someone before. It's pissing me off. I've tried fucking other people the last few months, and all it's done is make me want him more, because no one else compared to what it was like with him.

"Here, I'll get you started," Matt says, and moves over to

my nightstand. He opens it and takes out the box of condoms, a couple of different dildos, a prostate massager, and a bottle of lube, and then moves back over to the suitcase and drops them inside. "There, that's the essentials. You can do the rest." He grins at me and I can't help smiling.

"Thanks," I say.

"Don't mention it. I'll be back in thirty minutes to make sure you're actually packed." He pats my shoulder and walks away.

I take a deep breath and let it out, then move to my dresser. Besides the fact that Mom wants me to meet her fiancé, Oliver, I also don't have a job right now since the bar I work at, *Dave's*, is having some renovations done and is closed for the next month. Honestly it's the perfect time for me to go home. Fortunately, even with the lack of a job I'm still getting paid.

"Time's up!" Matt calls twenty five minutes later, as he wanders into my room for the second time.

I turn to him and gesture to my fully packed suitcase, even managing a smile. Then tuck the hair that has slid out of my messy bun behind my ear. He grins at me.

"Good, now get lost. Scram, skedaddle, and don't come back without having used all the supplies in that suitcase."

I roll my eyes as I head towards the front door. "Tell Sam I say goodbye and I'll see you guys in a month?"

"Sure thing, man," Matt says, and waves as I close the door behind me.

An hour later, I'm pulling into the driveway of my childhood home. A two story with light blue siding and white brick, and a wood burning fireplace and hardwood floors throughout. It's not huge, but it was perfect for Mom and me. Three bedrooms and two and half bathrooms. Cozy and quaint. The bedroom downstairs is used as an office, while the Master bedroom and my bedroom are on the second floor.

I take a deep breath as I prepare myself to meet this Oliver guy, who apparently swept Mom off her feet in a short amount of time. We don't talk on the phone a ton, but when we do she gushes over him, and I know they've been living together since they got engaged, maybe even before that, so I'm expecting him to be here.

I'm trying to stay positive, to put on a good face and give this guy a chance. If Mom likes him he must be decent. And she hasn't been married before. My sperm donor father knocked her up and disappeared, so it's just been the two of us since, and while she's dated, she never found a guy who actually appreciated her intelligence and hard work. Until now, I guess.

The last thing I want to do is rain on their parade, no matter how miserable I feel. It's not about me. So I climb out of my car, determined to be happy for them, and grab my suitcase from the trunk.

Trudging up the driveway in the thousand degree July heat, I make my way up the steps and turn the doorknob. "Mom!" I call, stopping just inside the doorway and closing the door behind me.

"Hunter?" Mom says from in the kitchen, then races in to throw her arms around me in a tight hug. I smile and hug her back, drinking in the scent of her lemon and raspberry body wash. I hug her tighter. I didn't realize how much I needed a hug until I got one. "It's so good to see you," she coos.

"You, too," I say, pulling away.

"Thank you for coming. It really means a lot to both of us. Come meet Oliver. He's in the kitchen." I nod and follow her through the living room and towards the back of the house.

When I stop in the doorway to the kitchen I halt and my heart rate skyrockets. I must be seeing things, but from the back he looks just like—

"Amanda, love, where's the basil for the sauce?" I hear in

a voice that sounds scarily familiar. My heart is pounding now as blood rushes to my ears.

"Oliver," Mom says, and he turns. The blood drains from my face as I stare at cobalt eyes, auburn hair, and a freckle-scattered face. He's staring back at me with the same bewilderment on his face that I'm sure is present on mine, before he steels himself and holds out his hand.

"Hello," he greets me like we've never met before. Like he wasn't moaning underneath me three fucking months ago. Like he didn't beg me to fuck him and then fucking leave my aparment without a word the next morning. Rage ignites inside me, quickly followed by terror and disgust as I realize there's no way he wasn't cheating on Mom that night.

The fucking bastard. Mom is crazy about this guy and he's a two timing son of a bitch, who lied to me, and fuck, I slept with my mother's boyfriend.

"Nice to meet you, *Oliver*," I say, enunciating his name harshly, and he flinches as I shake his hand, squeezing hard enough that hopefully it hurts, before I turn back to Mom. "I'm not feeling so well all of a sudden. I think I'm going to go lay down for a while."

"Oh, okay," she says. "We'll save you some dinner. Oliver is a wonderful cook."

"Oh, I bet he is," I say under my breath, before heading around the hall and up the stairs to my old room, shutting the door behind me. I grip a pillow off the bed and hold it to my face before I fucking scream.

$$Four$$

OLIVER

"You okay?" Amanda asks as we sit at the dinner table, eating the pasta dish I baked for us for when Hunter arrived. It's a staple of mine, one of my favorites, and since Amanda told me Hunter loves pasta, that's what I went with. Something to make his first time back home in a while a little bit nicer, to perhaps ease the fact that his mother was getting married to me in two month's time. A man he had never met.

Except he had.

Turning around to see him standing there, the boy I hadn't been able to stop thinking about since that night, who had invaded every moment of my existence the last three months, who was making it harder and harder to convince myself that marrying a woman was what I wanted, that what we had done was just a change of pace, was the last thing I expected. It was killing me, knowing that he was Amanda's son.

Hunter.

No, I was not okay right now. I was very far from okay. I knew he had put two and two together and realized that when we'd fucked it had been during the time that his mother and I were an item.

God, how could I be so stupid? But I had no way of knowing that Hunter was the boy who'd had me so utterly captivated, so smitten, so enthralled, so wanting, that I had let myself do something I never imagined I would do.

Hunter, the beautiful, sexy, young man who had done things to me that I had only ever dreamt about. Amanda's son. My fiancée's son.

How could this be happening? How could things have gone so disastrously wrong to end up here? Would Hunter say something to his mother? We were supposed to be leaving for a road trip in only a few days. How were we going to be in such close quarters with each other, traveling together, and pretend like we hadn't fucked? Twice. Like he hadn't turned my world upside down.

Bloody hell.

"I'm fine, darling," is my answer, as I pick at my meal, my stomach in knots, nausea building. I've got a tension headache brewing as well. Reaching for my water glass, I take a sip and will it to help me settle, even the tiniest bit.

"Dinner is really good," she replies, taking another bite. "I'm sorry Hunter couldn't join us."

"It's quite alright," I tell her. "I'm sure he's tired. We'll have plenty of time together over the next month."

She nods and reaches over to squeeze my hand. I manage a small smile. "We've got the RV rental secured. I'll be at the office until the day we leave, so if you and Hunter want to pick it up?"

I nod. "Of course." I've never been in an RV before, so it should be an experience. Normally I would just stay at a hotel, but Amanda assures me it's a wonderful way to vacation, and enjoy the different camp sites, and I am up for trying something new. Besides, she told me this was how she and Hunter used to vacation and she wanted to make it enjoyable for him.

How enjoyable will it be, I wonder, if I'm along?

We finish our meal and load the dishes into the dishwasher. Amanda turns on the water and starts to wash the pots and pans. "You want to go check on Hunter while I finish up here?" she asks. "See if he's up for eating anything before we pack up the leftovers?"

The severity of my headache is increasing at the thought, my stomach knotting further, but I nod, and make my way up the stairs to Hunter's room. Fuck, I'm shaking like a leaf as I reach up and knock on the door lightly. "Hunter?" I say, trying to keep my voice from shaking as well as I say his name for the first time. "Your mother sent me to ask if you would like to eat yet?"

When there's no answer, I sigh, and twist the knob, slowly opening the door and peeking inside. Hunter is lying on his side, facing away from me, his phone in his hand. Only the lamp on the nightstand illuminates his frame.

"Hunter?" I say again quietly. "Would you like to eat?" I want to talk to him. I want to apologize to him, to tell him I never intended for this to happen, to try and explain. But I don't. What is there to explain? I fucked up, and he unwittingly was party to it. How he must hate me. I can't blame him at all, because I fucking hate myself. Though I don't know if there's ever been a time where that wasn't the case.

He doesn't turn to look at me. "No, thank you."

"There's plenty of leftovers if you change your mind," I say, and then shut the door before making my way back downstairs.

I watch a movie with Amanda, the entire time lost in thoughts of Hunter, of Amanda, of how I've inadvertently ruined their relationship with each other, all because of my greed, stupidity, and selfishness. Because of my lack of self control, my own desires, and curiosities. The one time I actually let myself be reckless, let myself indulge, and it's come back to bite me in the arse more than I ever even considered possible.

Even if Amanda never finds out about Hunter and I, things will undoubtedly never be the same between them again. I've put him in an impossible situation. The honorable thing to do would be to confess everything to her and leave Hunter out of it. He didn't know who I was, and while I didn't know who he was either, I did know I was cheating. But the thought of saying anything terrifies me, and the thought of Mother and Father finding out, of the wedding being canceled, is enough to make my heart rate spike and sweat break out on my forehead. This wedding is all I have left. It's my last hope, the lifeline to keep me from drowning. If I can marry Amanda I can forget all of these ridiculous fantasies of being with a man. Everything will fall into place.

Hunter doesn't come out for the rest of the night, and when Amanda and I make our way up to our own room across the hall from his, the faint light from underneath his doorway is gone completely, telling us he's asleep.

When Amanda curls up with her head on my chest I tell myself the same thing I've been telling myself for months now. *It's for the best.* Amanda is kind, intelligent, hard working, beautiful, and she puts up with my parents. She's everything a man could want. Exactly the kind of woman my parents expected me to marry.

When she leans up and kisses me, I kiss her back, but I can't help thinking about how her son's lips felt against mine. Free of make up. Fuller, the bottom lip slightly more so than the top, the smell of his peppermint breath and the orange scent wafting off of him that I've clung to, all these months later. I never thought I would see him again, and now that he's across the hall from me I don't know what to do. And even though guilt and shame wash over me, I can't keep my thoughts from straying to him when Amanda's hand slides down my pants, wishing it was his hand around my cock.

When she wraps her lips around my erection it's his hair I want to grab on to, his eyes that I want looking up at me. When I come moments later it's his name that I have to keep from falling from my lips.

It's for the best, I tell myself over and over again, as I drift to sleep with her in my arms.

HUNTER

When I wake up, it's daylight, and the sun is splashing light across the room. Rolling over slowly, I check my phone and see it's nine o'clock. Mom will be at work and hopefully so will Mr. Two-Timing Bastard.

I groan and place a hand over my eyes as I try to reconcile myself with the knowledge that the man I haven't been able to stop thinking about for three months is in my house, marrying my mother in only two months.

What the actual fuck? Logically I know there's no way I could have known it was him when we slept together. Neither one of us gave our names, I had never seen a picture of him. He never bothered to fucking tell me he had a girl-friend. I never would have fucked him if I'd known. I know this isn't on me.

But then another thing occurs to me. They've been engaged for almost three months. Did he go out and propose to her the very next day? What the actual hell? I'm so fucking pissed off, confused and hurt I don't know where to start. Was he just using me as one last hurrah before he asked Mom to marry him? How fucked up is that? I want to strangle him for putting me in the middle of this against my knowledge, for making me think he cared, even a little bit, for spending so much energy and time thinking about him. I can't believe I shed tears over the asshole. And how can I let Mom marry someone who was unfaithful to her? Does she know? Should I say something? I don't know how to do that without ruining everything.

My stomach grumbles and I have to pee, so I guess I should start there.

Sliding out of bed, I make my way to the bathroom across the hall in my pajama bottoms and no shirt. I pee, wash my hands, run my fingers through my hair before tying it back in a messy bun, and then make my way downstairs to the kitchen for breakfast and coffee. It's quiet, thank God. I could use the time to myself, away from Mom and Oliver to figure things out. Like how the hell I'm supposed to go on a two week long road trip with them, watching Oliver share a bed with Mom, watch them kiss and flirt and hold hands, while I try to pretend like nothing happened between us. I'm so pissed that I slam my coffee mug down on the counter before getting a k cup out and placing it in the Keurig. I turn it on and wait for it to warm up before setting my mug under the dispenser and pushing the button.

"Good morning," I hear and start, turning to see Oliver standing there in slacks and a button down shirt, sleeves rolled up and the first couple of buttons undone. He looks exactly like he did the night we fucked. And even though I hate myself for it, I find I can't look away. He's too fucking pretty not to stare at.

"What the hell are you doing here?" I snarl, finally meeting his gaze, and remembering that I'm fucking furious with him. He flinches at my words. Good. If he thinks I'm going to be nice to him, pretend like nothing ever happened, like he didn't cheat on Mom, he's got another thing coming.

"I…I work from home," he says.

"Of course you fucking do." My words are bitter as I wait impatiently for my coffee so that I can get the fuck out of here. So much for enjoying my alone time. Looks like I'll either be stuck in my room all day or out doing I don't know what.

"Hunter," he says, in a way that has my chest squeezing, as he steps closer to me. I hold my hand up and shake my head.

"No," I say firmly. "Don't."

"It was a mistake," he continues, making my heart fall into my stomach. Don't I want him to admit that, though? To admit he was just stressed or overwhelmed, that he didn't mean to cheat on Mom? So why does it hurt so much? "I didn't—"

"No!" I shout, and I hate that I have tears stinging my eyes. I grab my coffee and even though I would normally be decorating it with cream and sugar, I take it black so I can get the fuck away from him.

When I reach my room, I slam the door and lock it behind me. He isn't worth my tears.

Unfortunately I'm still fucking starving even after I gag down the bitter coffee, but there's no way I'm going back downstairs.

Around seven that evening I hear a knock on my door. I've only left twice to go to the bathroom and shower, and other than that I've stayed put. I have my phone and a television, my video games, so I don't need to leave. But I'm so hungry now I feel sick.

"Hunter," I hear his sultry British voice, and my jaw clenches when a shiver runs down my spine. Fuck him. "Your mother won't be home until late. I made dinner if you want some. I'll be in my room so you can get it without worrying about running into me."

I wait until I hear him move across the hall and shut the door to the master bedroom. Then I slip out of my room and down the stairs to the kitchen where I pile my plate high with french fries and breaded fish. I moan when I'm back up in my room and stuffing my face. The man might be an absolute fuckwad, but he can cook.

I play video games for a while after my plate is clean, before I hear Mom's footsteps ascending the stairs, and there's an ache in my chest at the knowledge that she's sharing a bed with Oliver. That she's the one in his arms, that she's kissing him, touching him, being fucked by him. The man cheated, twice, and I hate him for it, but I also hate that he's in my house and I'm not allowed to touch him. He isn't mine. He will never be mine. How can I go the rest of my life with him as my stepfather when what I want is for him to be my lover? How can I still desire him when I know the kind of man he is? How can I sleep, knowing what's going on down the hall from me, between my mom and the only man who's ever made me want more than a one night stand?

How am I going to survive the next month, let alone the next thirty years, being in his presence and pretending I don't want him?

I turn my game off after another hour, then go across the hall to brush my teeth and use the bathroom, thankful that if anything is going on behind their closed door I can't hear it. I finish in the bathroom before returning to my room. I close my door and climb into bed. I lie there for several more hours before I finally fall asleep. And even then, it's restless.

<h1 style="text-align:center">Five</h1>

HUNTER

The next day I run some errands and pick up any last minute things we might need for our road trip. I bring everything inside and grab some lunch, before I make my way back up to my room.

My phone buzzes and I pull it out of my pocket as I sit on my bed. It's a group text with Matt and Sam.

Matt: Yo, dude, how's it going? What do you think of your mom's man??

God, that's a loaded question. He's a lying, cheating, son of a bitch, and the guy I've been hung up on for months, and I can't be around him without being furious and wanting him at the same time, and I have no idea if I should say something to Mom, because how can I tell her I slept with her boyfriend, even if I didn't know who he was, and break her heart, outing Oliver in the process? But how can I not, and let her marry someone who cheated on her? He put me in the worst, most fucked up situation of my life and I don't know what to do.

Me: Haven't decided yet.

Sam: lol, don't be too hard on him for banging your mom

Nausea fills my stomach and a surge of jealousy roils through me. I know that's messed up, but he was mine, goddamn it. Only for a night, but it was enough to make an imprint on me so deep I don't know how to think of him with Mom and not feel sick or fucking furious.

Me: Ewww, barfing emoji

Matt: lol, enjoy your road trip

Me: thanks

I toss my phone aside, the sandwich I'd made only ten minutes ago looking far less appetizing now. I shove it away and pick up my controller before drowning my feelings in a game of *Call of Duty*.

I've managed to avoid Oliver for the most part, over the past couple of days. We've run into each other occasionally, but I've spent most of my time in my room or out of the house. The worst time of day is in the evening, when Mom is home and we're expected to eat dinner together around the table like a fucking family.

The icing on the cake is when she tells us she might not be able to make it on the trip after all because of work. I can tell she feels awful about it, and she's exhausted. Apparently things are really hectic and intense right now with the case she's working on, and while she has someone who can cover for her that she trusts, she's worried it will be too much for them.

I can't be upset with Mom, though. She's always been amazing at what she does, and one of the things I respect about her is her dedication to her clients and helping them get the justice they deserve. She's clearly stressed, and warring with herself about whether or not she should be making the trip. But if she decides she can't come I'll just head back to my apartment because I am not going on the road for two weeks with just Oliver, or spending more time here alone with him, or I'm fairly certain I'll end up on the six o'clock news.

It's the second night in a row we've done the family meal thing now, and I always eat as quickly as possible so I can excuse myself. I hate doing it, because I don't want to be rude to Mom, but I can't stomach sitting across from Oliver and pretending like everything is okay. I tell her about my job when she asks, and about the classes I'll be taking next semester for my psychology major. I fill her in on my room-mates. When she asks if I'm seeing anyone I have to do my best not to glance at Oliver. "No," I say. "Not right now. There was someone I thought might turn into something but turns out he's a real prick and was just using me. He was in a rela-tionship the whole time."

I see Oliver flinch and his face flush out of the corner of my eye, and I can't help but feel a bit proud of myself for that one. He fuckling deserves it after what he did.

"Oh, my," Mom replies, clearly stunned. "Well, I'm glad you found out before it turned uglier."

I don't say anything, just finish my meal and head back to my room, telling her that I'm going to look through my things and decide what to pack for the trip we'll be leaving on the day after tomorrow, though I'm seriously considering telling her I can't make it, and making something up, like I need to get back to my apartment, or I'm not feeling well so I shouldn't be traveling. I wish I could use work as an excuse, but she already knows the bar is under construction so that won't work.

This fucked up situation and the lack of sleep I've been getting has me utterly exhausted and out of sorts. I'm so wiped out that I head to bed before ten o'clock. I'm out before my head hits the pillow.

"How long are you going to ignore me?" Fucking hell, this is the second time he's made me freak the fuck out while I'm minding my own goddamn business getting coffee.

"Well, let's see, the wedding is in two months, so, I'm thinking probably a good thirty or forty years, give or take," I say, stirring my cream into my coffee.

"Hunter, please." His voice is earnest. "You have to know I never meant to hurt you, or your mother."

I glare at him now. "Yes, you made it very clear that it was a "mistake" I say, putting the word in finger quotes. "Does she know?" He blinks at me. "Does she know, Oliver? Did you fucking tell my mom that you cheated on her? I'm not stupid, you know. I did the goddamn math. How long after you left before you proposed?"

His cheeks darken and he swallows. "It doesn't matter."

"It couldn't have been more than a week, Oliver! Was it the same fucking day? You rushed out of my apartment and you were so guilt ridden, you had to do whatever the fuck you could to make yourself feel better about it so you gave her a goddamn ring? Does she at least know you're not straight? Did you tell her that much?"

"I am—"

"If you end that sentence with anything other than "a fucking bastard" I will punch you in the nose," I grit out. "Don't you dare stand there and lie to me after what we did. You can fucking lie to yourself all you want, Oliver. You can lie to my mom if that's what you want, but don't you dare lie to me. I don't know why you are doing this. Why you are so determined to make everyone around you believe that you are something you aren't. But guess what? Putting a ring on Mom's finger doesn't change a goddamn thing, you asshole!" My cheeks are flaming and I'm definitely shouting, but the most horrifying thing about this whole exchange are the tears sliding down my cheeks. "You never told me you were in a relationship. I didn't even get the chance to make that choice, and now I have to pay for the consequences. Do you have any idea how hard it's been for me the past few days, being around her and pretending like everything between us is normal? Pretending I didn't—" My breath catches and I can't finish the words.

"Hunter," he says, stepping towards me again, but I back away as a whimper escapes me.

"I don't know what to do," I sob. "And the worst part is, I fucking cried over you, Oliver. Do you know that? The morning you left, without a word, after you told me you would stay, I fucking cried. And then I show up here and you fucking tell me it was a mistake. After I haven't been able to stop thinking about you, about us, jerking off to thoughts of us together night after night because that's all I have left. Thinking I would never see you again. And now here you are, and I can't..." My chest heaves. "I can't have you. Because you're marrying my mom."

He's close enough to me now that I can smell his ginger-bread and vanilla scent, and before I know it, he's taking me in his arms and holding me close to him as I sob, my arms wrapped around him, releasing so much hurt, and anger and grief that I'd bottled up not just since I got home and found out who he was, but since he left that morning three months ago.

"I'm so sorry," he whispers. "I'm so sorry, Hunter. I know I was wrong to leave. I didn't know what to do. I'm a complete bastard. I know that. I was scared. So very very scared at how utterly bewitched I was by you. I've made some very poor choices in my life, but you, Hunter Price, were not one of them. Even though it makes me the scum of the earth, I don't regret what we did, even for a second. I said it was a mistake because I had to convince myself it wasn't exactly what I wanted, to assuage my own guilt. I never intended to cheat on your mother. I've been telling myself I'm not gay for over twenty years, Hunter, because I can't be gay. Not in my family. Not with my parents. They would never accept it. Being anything other than straight is an unpardonable sin in their eyes and I've spent my entire life hearing about how vile it is, how unnatural. Marrying your mother seemed like the next best thing. Though truth be told it can't compare to how it felt being with you. I've done my best to live the only life I can, knowing I can never be who I really am. I had never been with another man before that night, though God knows I'd wanted it. Something about you made me so utterly reckless. I haven't stopped thinking about you either. Though, heaven knows I've tried."

I lift my head and stare at him. He brings his thumbs to my cheeks and wipes my tears.

"You want me?" It's subtle, but he nods.

"More than I care to admit." His finger reaches for the loose lock of hair that's fallen out of my messy bun and he tucks it behind my ear.

"What do we do?" I ask, feeling so torn inside I could scream.

"What do you want to do, sweet boy?" he asks me.

My heart thrashes against my rib cage. Then I'm gripping his cheeks and kissing him, hard. He moans, the sound vibrating throughout my entire body and making me shiver. Oh, God, yes. This is what I remember. This is what it felt like to have our lips locked and our tongues tangling. This is what I have been craving since the morning he walked away. I need this man. I need his kisses, his touch, his taste. I need his firm, hard body underneath me. I need my lips wrapped around his cock. I need his obedience, his surrender. I need to hear those sinful sounds pouring from his lips again and again.

"Hunter," he gasps, pulling away. His eyes flit to my lips and then back to my eyes. Then he's crashing his lips to mine again and pressing me up against the counter. He stands between my splayed thighs and we make out like we're fucking starving for each other, because we are. When I grip his auburn locks in my hand and tug, he whimpers and my cock jerks, aching for him.

"Fuck, I need to be inside you," I pant, between kisses.

"God, yes, please," is his reply. It sounds so desperate I nearly cry. I'm fully aware that there is no going back from this. That when we slept together the last time I was none the wiser and so can't be blamed for what happened. This time, though, I'm a willing participant. But the fact that this could absolutely destroy my relationship with my mother, who is the only fucking family I have, doesn't make me want to stop. I can't stop. I need him. He's mine. He's been mine since that first night. And I've been his.

"Strip and bend over the table," I tell him. My cock jerks when he begins to do exactly as I say, untucking his shirt, then unbuttoning it, before he moves to his belt. I slide my T-shirt and sweats off, then my underwear. When I look up again he's bent over the table just like I instructed, that gorgeous ass in the air, cock hard between his legs and leaking onto the floor.

In the light of day I can see the freckles scattered across his legs and ass, and I moan as I kneel behind him and spread his cheeks. "Fuck, I've missed this ass, Oli," I say, and he turns to look at me, his eyes wide.

"What is it?" I ask.

"Love it when you say my name while I'm bent over for you," he says, the huskiness in voice sending a shiver down my spine.

"Mmmm," I hum, then lick and nibble at his ass cheeks, making him jerk. "Oli," I say, planting kiss after kiss and nuzzling his delectable ass with my nose, repeating his name each time until he's shaking. "So good for me."

"Fuck," he gasps, as I reach my hand between his legs to fondle his balls. "Fuck, Hunter."

I hum again, then begin to suck on the freckles dotting his cheeks, making him spasm even more. I snarl when he says, "Fuck, don't leave marks, she'll see."

"You want me to fuck you and not mark you?" I say. I know he's right. This is reckless enough without leaving evidence on his body of what we're doing. But it fucking infuriates me that he's mine and I can't claim him the way I want to. I want him covered in my marks. His ass, his stomach, his neck. Every fucking place on his body belongs to me. Not her.

He looks back at me again. "Please?"

"On one condition. You tell me who's ass this is. Tell me it's mine and I won't mark it." His eyes widen again and I slap his ass cheek, making his cheeks flame and his eyes widen even further. "Tell me, Oli."

"I," he swallows. I slap his other ass cheek and he hisses. "Christ."

"Who's ass is this?" I ask more harshly. "Is it hers? Is it my mom's? Does your ass belong to her?"

He shakes his head. "Then whose is it, Oli?" I demand.

"Christ," he whimpers. "It's yours."

I press a kiss to it. "It's not hers?" Another kiss. He shakes his head vehemently. "You sure?" Another kiss, and a nod.

"Yes, now bloody fuck me, for Christ's sake," he almost snarls. I can't help chuckling as I spread his cheeks and begin to lap and suck at his beautiful pucker.

"God, Oli, you taste so good," I moan. "So fucking perfect, baby. Such a pretty hole. It hasn't been filled since I saw you last has it? Not even with a toy?" I reach around and grip his cock, both of us moaning at the contact.

He shakes his head. "N…no," he manages.

"Good boy," I purr, and his cock spasms in my hand. Holy fuck, he loved that. He loved being called my good boy.

"Damn, Oli," I purr, and he shoves his ass back, begging. "More. Please."

I hum and stroke my finger up and down his ass cheek. "Your hole must be aching to be filled," I say.

"Christ, you little demon, get the fuck inside me."

I slap his ass again and he gasps, then moans like a whore when I slide my tongue over his pucker again. "Oh, God. Yes, Hunter, fuck, yes, don't stop. Please don't stop. So good. So bloody good."

I slide my tongue over his taint and across his entrance

again and again, his taste exploding on my tongue, until he's shaking and I hear the hitch in his breath when he says, "Please," again. My cock is throbbing, desperate to be inside him. It's been too long. Way too long.

I moan and slip my tongue inside him, and he spasms around me. It's fucking glorious. I work him with my tongue as he presses back against me, fucking himself on my face.

I slide out of him and he whimpers as I ask, "You gonna keep denying this pretty hole what it needs?"

He shakes his head. "You gonna let me fill you up over and over again, Oli?"

A nod.

"You gonna let me take what I want when I fucking want, beautiful?" He nods again. I stand and look around for a substitute for lube since I don't have any on me.

"What are you doing?" he asks, looking over his shoulder as I move towards the cupboard above the stove. I grab the olive oil and return to him.

"Lube, beautiful." He nods and I cover my fingers in it before slicking up my cock. "You ready, gorgeous?" I ask.

"Christ, yes."

I align myself with his entrance, then plant kisses to his shoulder blades and along his neck as I grip his hips and press inside him. He hisses and I stroke his back. "You're okay," I promise. "You've got this, Oli. Just like the first time when you took me so well, remember?"

He takes a breath and lets it out, nodding his head, and I push past his tight ring, sliding inside him, his heat surrounding me, and we both groan. "God, that's good." I press more kisses to his sweaty back. "You okay?"

"Yes," he replies, his breathing heavy. "More."

"I'm coming, baby," I promise. "But I don't want to hurt you." He fucking squirms, and whimpers, and it's so damn hot my cock jerks inside him.

"Shit!" he cries. "Please, Hunter. I need you. All of you."

"Fuck, baby," I say on a groan. "You make me crazy, you

know that? Fucking love this perfect ass. So fucking hot watching it swallow my cock, Oli."

"Fuck," he moans as I bottom out. He's trembling, and I take a deep breath this time before I slide out a little bit and push back in, then slide out even more, before pushing back in again.

"Shit!" he cries out when I peg his prostate. "Shit, that's good. Harder." I repeat the motion, hearing his moans and the sound of our breaths, skin slapping against skin as I pound into him again and again. The salt and pepper shakers on the table tumble over, their contents spilling out, and the table scooches slightly across the floor.

"Fuck, baby, you feel so damn good," I growl. "Touch yourself, beautiful. I'm gonna make you come so fucking hard."

He grips his cock and I snap my hips again and again, making him cry out. Pleasure zings down my spine and my body shakes. My balls are aching. "I'm so fucking close," I tell him, then slide my arm around his middle and haul him up so that his back is against my chest and he's impaled on my cock. Then I grip his cock over his hand as I shove up into him and stroke him at the same time.

"Oh, Christ," he wails. "I'm going to come."

"Yes," I tell him. "Come for me, Oli. Be good and come hard for me." He howls as his release spills all over our hands and onto the table, and I'm crying out seconds later as his ass clenches around me, my cock spasming as I unload my spunk inside him. Fuck, that was intense, and so damn good.

I bring my hand to his mouth. "Clean it off."

His tongue darts out and he licks up his own release greedily, sucking my fingers into his mouth and moaning around them, making my cock jerk inside him yet again.

"So good for me," I tell him, and watch as his cheeks flush. I press a kiss to his shoulder.

"Shit," I say, wincing as I pull out of him. I bite my lip. My release is sliding down his perfect thighs, which is hot as hell, but it makes me realize my mistake.

"What?" he says, his breaths still heavy.

"I forgot a condom. Fuck, Oli, I'm sorry. I got so caught up in the moment, and I didn't think. That was stupid."

"Even stupider to let it go to waste," he says, surprising me. I return to my knees and lap the cum from his ass and thighs and he moans again.

"Come here," I say, standing, and he turns. I press my mouth to his and let my taste fill his mouth as I kiss him. He grips my cheeks and moans as his tongue slides over mine.

"Christ, what am I going to do with you?" he says, reaching up and brushing that stray strand of hair behind my ear again. "You almost make me believe that what I want is within reach."

"And what's that?" I say, as his hand cups my cheek.

He gives me a sad smile. "Happiness."

I frown. "You don't have to marry her, Oli, if she doesn't make you happy. You *shouldn't* marry her."

"It's all right," he says. "I could do far worse than your mother."

"Do you love her?" I ask, staring into his eyes.

He sighs. "I care for her, Hunter. Love will come with time."

I shake my head, stepping away. "Are you kidding me? What a load of bull."

"Hunter—"

"No, Oliver, that's not how sexuality works. You can't marry someone to fucking hide who you are and hope you'll eventually love them. And what, to appease some homophobic assholes? Is that what you want? To go through the rest of your life in a loveless marriage? To always be catering to what your parents want instead of what you want?"

"What I want doesn't matter, Hunter!" he bellows, and I step back further, eyes wide. "I have no desire to hurt anyone.

Least of all you or your mother. But it isn't about what I desire. It's about doing what's best for my family."

"Bullshit," I say, tears stinging at the corners of my eyes, as I point my finger at him. "It's about protecting yourself. And hiding behind my mom, because you're too damn scared to upset Mommy and Daddy. Fuck, I was so stupid." I grab my underwear and sweats off the kitchen floor and slide them back on.

"Hunter—"

"I'm going to take a shower," I say, and hurry out of the kitchen.

I have more tears sliding down my cheeks as I scrub and rinse, then dry off and head to my room to change. I tie my hair back in a messy bun again before I sit on my bed.

Fuck, I don't know what I expect from him. He doesn't owe me anything. He's not in love with me either. And I don't know the kind of family obligations he has or the kind of pressure he's under. My coming out was simple, easy. I told Mom, and my friends at school, and it was never a big deal. Sure being queer hasn't been a cake walk but I've always known it was who I was and I was never ashamed of it. I never had a reason to be.

But Oliver doesn't have that support. It sounds like his parents have done everything to discourage him from being himself. Told him time and time again that being gay is unacceptable, to the point where he is marrying a woman to hide who he is. Maybe even to convince himself he isn't gay. Fuck, that's messed up. And as furious as I am with him, I also can't help feeling sorry for him. He's buried who he is for twenty years because he's so terrified of shaming and disgracing his family. It makes me want to punch his parents in their stuck up, homophobic noses and make them realize what an incredible son they have. He's trying so hard to make everyone else happy, he's given up on his own happiness. Well, maybe I can make him happy, for a little while at least.

When I hear the water turn on in the master bathroom I

decide it's time to pay him another visit. He made a promise to me and I intend to take him up on it.

When I enter the bathroom and my gaze lands on Oliver's naked form behind the glass door of the shower, my cock springs back to life. I watch as the water pours over his lithe body, sliding over his freckled shoulders and down his toned back, over the swell of his perfectly round ass. I moan and strip off my clothes before I open the shower door and step inside.

OLIVER

I start when I hear the shower door opening, but don't have a chance to turn around before a wet, naked body is pressed up against my backside and a familiar voice rumbles in my ear, "Did you mean it, Oliver, when you told me I could fill you whenever I wanted?"

I shiver at his words, and his touch. I nod. "Yes," I reply in almost a whisper.

He reaches around me and takes my semi hard cock in his hand, then begins to stroke it as I close my eyes and moan at the sensation. "Let me make you happy, Oli," he says. "For one month." He nibbles on my ear, sending a shiver down my spine and making my cock ooze precum as it hardens in his grip. Then his lips move to my shoulders, and my upper back. "I have one month here, with you before I go back to school, and work. Let me spend it making you happy."

I nod. "God, yes. Use me. Fill me, Hunter. I'm yours." He plants kisses on my shoulder blade as he continues to stroke me. My hands come up to rest on the shower wall as I moan, and pant, feeling his rock hard cock against my arse. "I want to give you all of your firsts, Oli," he murmurs before I feel a slick finger sliding inside my hole. He doesn't stretch me. No, I don't need that since we fucked only half an hour ago. Instead he slides in and pegs my prostate, making me jerk up to my tiptoes. "Fuck!" I cry out. He doesn't let up, just nudges that deliciously sensitive spot over and over and I'm so close to orgasm again I don't know if I can hold back. But then his finger slips free and I find myself whimpering at the loss and the intense desire to come.

"Turn around," he orders, and I do. He immediately grips my wrists and pins them above my head, and Christ my cock jerks like crazy. Why the hell do I love that so damn much? More precum slides down my shaft as he steps closer and grips both of our cocks, his eyes lust filled and his cheeks flushed. "Mmmm," he hums, as he presses kisses to my jaw and neck while he strokes us in tandem. "I've missed this big, beautiful cock, Oli." Christ, the things he says. I may come just from listening to that filthy mouth.

He presses kiss after kiss to my wet skin and strokes us so torturously slow it'll be hours before I come, but I will never lose my erection. The friction of his cock against mine is magnificent. "Please," I whimper, thrusting into his grip. He chuckles, then presses a kiss to my lips.

"So pretty when you beg, Oli."

"Christ, I'll beg you to make me come over and over again if you want it," I tell him. "Just to have any part of you on me, or inside me. Just tell me to beg and I will." His eyes flare and he strokes us faster, making me let out a guttural moan. "Fuck, that's good." I want to reach down and grip his hair, or his shoulders, anything, but he's holding me in place tightly, and the fact that I can't get free is turning me on even more as my cock leaks precum like crazy, sliding down my shaft and over his hand. The fact that he has his hand around my rock hard cock while he pins me in place is so unbeliev-ably hot.

"Christ, I'm going to come." His grip on my wrists tightens at the same time as the grip on my cock does and I explode into his hand, my cock pulsing my release. He lets go of me and uses my cum as lube as he continues to stroke himself while I watch. It's the hottest thing I've ever seen, and I feel my dick twitching again, trying to spring back to life for the third time when his head snaps back and he cries out, as his cock spasms in his grip and he shoots all over his stomach and hand.

"Bloody hell," I gasp, still catching my breath. He licks his own release from his hand, and I moan. Then he steps closer and kisses me again, letting the taste of him slide from his mouth to mine. I moan as his spunk lands on my tongue and I swallow it down. God, he's delicious. I run my fingers through those beautiful locks, as our tongues tangle. Then we take the time to wash each other off before stepping out of the shower and slipping our clothes back on.

When he pulls me towards his room I don't hesitate. We climb onto his bed and he snuggles up against me, resting his head on my chest.

"This okay?" he asks, and I nod as I comb my fingers through his hair, the dampness of it making my own shirt wet, but I don't care. We lie in silence for a moment before he speaks.

"Why didn't you tell me it was your first time with a man that night? I would have made it good for you."

I lift his chin so he's looking up at me and press a kiss to his lips. "You did," I tell him sincerely. "It was everything I dreamed it would be. You were perfect, Hunter."

He kisses me this time and we don't part for quite some time. The kissing isn't hurried or rushed. It's soft, slow, and tender, and so utterly perfect. Christ, what this boy does to me.

"Don't you need to get back to work?" he asks, pulling away.

I shake my head. "I took the afternoon off to get ready for the trip."

He grins and rests his head back on my chest. "Do you like being an accountant?" he asks.

"You know what I do?" I say, surprised. "I never told you."

"Mom mentioned it, I think."

I nod. "Truthfully, no, I hate it."

"Why do you do it then?" he asks, tilting his head up to look at me.

"Because my father was paying for my education and my housing, and insisted I go into a worthwhile vocation. It was either this, or being a doctor or a lawyer. Neither of those suited me. I am good with money, but I don't enjoy it. I hate being stuck inside all day and sitting at a desk. It's never been me. Though I can't complain about the wages."

"What would you do if you had a choice?"

I bite my lip and he smiles. "What? Tell me."

"Promise you won't laugh?" I ask, and he bites his lip this time. "You're already laughing," I say, but I'm chuckling as I do, and poking his ribs. He shrieks and cackles and it's the most beautiful thing I've ever heard. His laugh is vibrant and absolutely lovely, and it makes my chest ache with fondness.

"Come on," he says, after I've stopped tickling him, his cheeks rosy and his eyes sparkling. "I promise I'll be good."

"I've always loved the outdoors," I say. "I love nature, and working with my hands, the idea of bringing something to life, letting it grow and flourish, do what it's meant to do. But I also really love the aesthetic side of things and seeing how things come together to compliment each other. I'd spend hours as a kid, just looking at gardening or landscaping magazines and books at the library. I still do sometimes. I'd love to get a job in landscaping, or possibly at a nursery, taking care of plants. I really love the idea of designing the landscaping, though."

"Really?" he says. I nod.

"Mmmm," he hums, running his finger down my chest. "I can see this beautiful body out in the sun and dirt, sweaty and sexy as fuck. Doing all that bending over."

I laugh. "I think you've watched a little too much porn."

He laughs, too, but then his voice is soft when he says, "I think that's really beautiful, Oli. I like hearing you talk about something that clearly makes you happy. Your dad didn't like that idea? The landscaping?"

"He was horrified when I told him. As if I had said I wanted to work on porta potties. Told me no son of his was going to be crawling around in the dirt for a living, that I needed to get my head on straight, and find a job that would actually allow me to take care of a family some day and not be a disgrace to the Jones' name."

"Shit, he sounds like a real charmer," Hunter remarks, and I chuckle.

"He's something, alright." I tuck a stray strand of hair behind his ear and he presses his lips to mine again.

"Tell me about your family," he says once he's pulled away and his head is resting against my chest once more.

I sigh as I continue to stroke my fingers through his hair. "Both my parents come from money. My father is an anesthesiologist who grew up in London and went to the finest schools. His father was a doctor. A renowned brain surgeon actually, and his mother was a famous model. He met my mother in college, and she dropped out after two years to get married. A couple of years after that my twin sister and I came along."

"You have a twin?" he asks, looking up at me yet again.

I nod. "Olivia. And a nephew, Freddie."

"Are they homophobic, too?"

I pause, thinking about how Olivia stood up to Mother when we were there that night I met Hunter. How she defended the gay boy Mother was gossiping about. And the way she looked at me afterwards, and asked if I was okay. I think about the phone call we had after I proposed to Amanda, when she asked if this was what I really wanted. We never talked about it growing up. I just assumed she shared our parents' opinions. Why wouldn't she? We'd both had it ingrained in us since childhood just how disgusting and perverse being gay was. How it was a stain on a family's name. An egregious sin.

I've wanted to say something to my parents for ages, but I never found the courage. Yet every time I didn't I felt a piece of me being smothered. Felt myself pulling that closet door a little bit tighter each time. I've never felt like I could be honest with anyone in my family about the questions I had in regard to my sexuality, because I'd been sitting at that dinner table for thirty-six years hearing my parents' comments and knowing that if I let it slip that I might be interested in men, if I ever acknowledge the fact that I might not be straight, I could lose everything. Facing their wrath, their disdain, their disappointment. Seeing the disgusted looks on their faces. I didn't know how to do that. I wasn't brave like Olivia was.

"I don't know," I say. "Maybe not."

"Maybe she would accept you. Maybe you wouldn't have to lose everything."

"Maybe," I say, and kiss his hair. "I'm still not sure I've fully accepted it myself yet. I've spent so long denying any attraction to men because I didn't want it to be true, I don't really know how to be the me that I've kept hidden for so long. I don't know how to be okay with that version of myself." Tears fill my eyes and my chest heaves slightly. He pushes up and looks at me, and I blink as he wipes the tears from my cheeks.

"I'm sorry you don't have the parents you deserve," he says. "I'm sorry you felt like living a lie was safer than being yourself. You don't have to pretend with me, Oli. You can be whoever you are. You're safe with me."

I bring his face to mine and kiss him deeply, because his words mean more than I can say. And I believe him. For the first time in my life I know someone sees me for who I really am, or at least who I want to be, and they accept me for me.

We doze and when we wake again it's late afternoon. I reach over and grab Hunter's phone off the nightstand to check the time. Shit, Amanda will be home soon and Hunter and I need to pick the RV up before five.

"Hey," I say, sliding my finger along his arm. "Wake up, we have to get going."

He grunts and shifts away from me, opening his eyes. "What time is it?"

"Four," I say. "We need to be at the RV place by five, and your mother will be home by six."

He frowns, and his gaze is earnest when he asks, "Will you fuck her tonight?"

Fuck, I never stopped to think about how difficult this would be for him. Watching me with his mother, especially when it'll be just the three of us in close quarters for the next two weeks. I won't be fucking her in front of him, of course, but I will be kissing her, touching her. I have to or she'll know something's up. And not having sex with her for the time we're on the road trip is doable. We really can't do anything with Hunter sharing the RV with us anyway, but what about afterwards when we get back home?

"Christ, Hunter, are you sure you want this? Perhaps it would be better if you went home early?"

His frown deepens. "You said I could have your hole whenever I wanted."

I press a kiss to his nose. "And I meant it, sweet boy, but I don't want you upsetting yourself when something happens between your mother and me, because I will fuck her while you are here, and I don't want to see you get hurt."

"I'll hurt for you, Oli. I said I would make you happy for a month and I meant it." He kisses me. "But you will hurt for me, too."

My eyes widen and he grins. "Just promise me you will think of me when you're inside her," he says, his eyes softer again. "Promise me when you come it will be because you pictured me inside you, filling you up and splitting you open. Being my good boy."

My cock jerks and I almost whimper. Why does that affect me the way it does? "I promise," I say, dumbfounded at how much I mean it, and he captures my lips again.

"Take off your pants," he rumbles.

"What? We need to leave or we'll be late. And I came twice in thirty minutes. I don't have the same refractory period you do, sweetheart."

"Oh, you're not coming, beautiful," he says. "Just me. I'm gonna use your pretty little hole to get off, and you're gonna lay there and take it like the good boy you are." He runs his fingers through my hair and I shudder.

"Christ, the mouth on you," I whisper, stroking his bottom lip with my thumb. "You could tell me to do anything and I would."

He smirks. "Then take your pants off, beautiful. And spread those pretty legs."

Six

OLIVER

Hunter and I are in the kitchen making dinner together a couple of hours later, having returned from the RV rental place only thirty minutes before, and stealing a few quick kisses before we can't anymore, when we hear the front door open and the thud of Amanda's shoes and bag hitting the floor.

"Oliver?" she calls, and she sounds exhausted. "Hunter?"

"In here, love!" I say, and she appears in the doorway a moment later, looking even worse than she sounded, her face drawn and circles under her eyes, but managing a smile as she looks from me to Hunter and back again.

"You alright?" I ask. She sighs and comes to me when I open my arms. I hold her as she rests her head on my chest. The guilt I feel over being with someone as incredible as her and not being satisfied is immeasurable. What is wrong with me? Amanda is not a bad woman. No, far from it. She's actually an amazing woman. And I hate that she doesn't make me happy, that I don't find myself sexually attracted to her, that I have to picture naked men when we fuck because it's the only thing that gets me hard, and she has no idea. No idea she's agreed to marry a man who can never love her the way she deserves. Admitting that to myself is huge. Because I've spent the last three months telling myself I can satisfy her, and she can satisfy me, when in reality I know better. But I'm so utterly terrified. Terrified of the truth. Terrified of myself, of what it means.

This is easier. I've been playing this game my entire life. I've done it for so long now I've almost convinced myself I actually could be happy with a woman. Especially one like her. One who, on top of being intelligent, beautiful, and kind, also knows how to handle my parents. When they brought up children literally a second after I introduced them, she wasn't upset, or dismissive. She just smiled and said, "We'll see what happens." And while I know that she has no desire to have another child, that answer kept my parents from bringing it up again.

Why is it so hard for me, as a thirty-six year old man, to be honest with my parents? So much so that I would risk not only my happiness, but hers as well? That I've stooped to sleeping with her son to get what she can never give me? Is this how it will always be for us? Me stepping out on her to fulfill some unmet need, her never being the wiser? I'd convinced myself I could be content with her, but having Hunter here is making me question that all over again. Damn him for showing up two fucking months before my wedding and turning my world upside down for a second time.

"Long day," Amanda says with a weary sigh. "Dinner smells amazing though. What did you guys make?"

"Salmon, rice, and asparagus," Hunter says, turning to her with a smile that looks very genuine.

"My boys, cooking for me," she croons. "You're both so amazing." She kisses me and then steps towards Hunter and kisses his cheek. "I'm gonna go change and I'll be right back."

She leaves and we exchange glances. I've carried guilt and shame like a weighted blanket around me for years. Before, because of my attraction to men, now because of what Hunter and I are doing. But I can't make myself stop. And somehow, being with him makes the pain a little bit more bearable, because he knows the real me, and maybe that takes a small fraction of the weight off of me. When he's inside me, when he tells me I'm good, I can almost believe him. Believe that I'm not broken, that who I am isn't an abomination, or an utter disgrace. That I deserve to be loved. To be happy.

"I have to tell you both something," she says, when she returns, wearing sweats and a T-shirt, her dark hair up in a ponytail instead of falling loosely over her shoulders like it was when she got home. She looks comfortable, but sad, and completely worn out.

"Everything alright, Mom?" Hunter asks as she sits at the table.

"I'm so sorry to do this at the last minute," she says, looking back and forth between us, "but I just couldn't make up my mind and I was really hoping maybe something would happen that would make me feel more at ease about leaving, but..." She bites her lip. "The trial got moved up, and, you know how much I want to make this trip, but I just can't afford to take time off work right now. I need to be here, doing the best I can for my client. So would you two be comfortable going without me? If you don't want to go I understand, but I hate to have you cancel because of me, and this was the main reason we asked Hunter to come home in the first place."

She looks at me now and takes my hand, squeezing it. "And I know you've been looking forward to it." I feel like a complete bellend that rather than be disappointed she's missing out, all I feel is excitement at the prospect of spending the next two weeks alone with Hunter. "I feel awful."

I chuckle slightly and stroke her cheek, before planting a kiss on her forehead. "It's all right, love. Hunter and I will be fine. It will give us time to get to know each other. We haven't had much the past few days with me working. I'm sure we'll manage."

She gives a sad smile, then kisses my hand. "Thank you. Be sure and send me pictures, huh?"

"Sure, Mom," Hunter says, as we sit down to eat.

HUNTER

I wait until I hear the front door closing and Mom's car starting the next morning, before I climb out of bed and use the bathroom. I brush my teeth, then wait a few more minutes just to be sure she isn't coming back, before I make my way down the hall to the master bedroom.

I know I should feel disappointed that she isn't coming with us on this trip, but all I feel is an intense giddiness at the idea of being alone with Oliver for the next two weeks, on the road, sharing an RV, going wherever we want to go and doing whatever we want to do. At first, the thought of Mom not being on this trip, of being alone with Oliver for two weeks, gave me hives, but now, after everything yesterday, it feels like a gift. I'm desperate for more time with him.

I do feel badly that Mom is so worn out and stressed. For her sake I wish things were less hectic, but I can't bring myself to wish she was coming, no matter how awful of a son that makes me. I only have a month with Oliver, and that time had dwindled down to two weeks, after spending time on the road and watching he and Mom touching and kissing, and I honestly didn't know how I was going to handle that, but I don't have to, now, and I'm not going to waste the time we have.

I turn the knob on the door and push it open to see him lying in the bed on his stomach, gripping the pillow, one leg sprawled out, his auburn hair a tousled mess, his back rising and falling as he breathes. He looks absolutely delicious and utterly fuckable. I'm overcome with an intense desire to fuck him in the bed he shares with Mom. To give him more pleasure there than she ever has or ever could. To have the sheets wrapped in my scent, to have him begging me, moaning for me, saying my name in the place where they've made love countless times. I want the last person he derives pleasure from in this bed to be me, not her.

Grabbing the lube from the nightstand, I strip my clothes off and climb onto the bed. There's a pang in my chest, and I know it's my conscience, telling me that this is wrong, but I push it down. I know I should feel guilty, that what I'm doing is despicable, but any remorse I feel is buried under the weight of my desire for him. My need for him. He's mine. I don't know how I'm going to walk away after this month is over and act like he doesn't own my heart, because he's already starting to, and I know it's inevitable. I can't stop this, the way he makes me feel when I'm inside him, the way he responds to me, the way he lets me take control.

His brokenness calls to me. His tenderness. His softness. His desire to be loved and accepted. To be good. He is so good. So beautiful. So perfect. And I will tell him that over and over again until he believes it.

Reaching his side, I pull the covers back and see that he's only in his underwear. I tug the waistband down and he squirms, the movement actually making it easier for me to undress him. I slide the underwear down as he turns his head to the other side, eyes still closed. Then I begin to nibble at his ass cheeks, and he squirms more, moaning slightly. I slide his underwear all the way off, then reach up and grip his half hard cock in my hand. His eyes flutter open as he moans, but then jerks as he realizes who is touching him.

"Shh," I sooth, pressing kisses to his back and then his neck. "She's gone."

He relaxes under my touch, his eyes closing again as I continue to press kisses down his spine and along his ass cheeks, nibbling and sucking as I stroke him. His cock feels so fucking incredible, hard and heavy, precum sliding down the sides and onto my hand. "Fucking love your cock, baby," I tell him, and he whimpers as his cock spasms in my grip. Fuck, that's hot. "You love when I tell you how good you are, don't you, Oli? How pretty you are? How goddamn fucking perfect?" His cock spasms again, harder, and I squeeze the base to stave off his orgasm. Fuck, I'm definitely making it a goal of mine to make him come just from praising him. But not today.

He whimpers when my hand leaves his cock. It's red and angry and so damn hard, my mouth is watering wanting to taste it again. But that will have to wait too.

He jerks again when I spread his ass cheeks and circle his pucker with a lubed finger. It flutters at my touch, and I groan. I don't want to stretch him much this time. I want him to fucking feel me. I slide my finger inside him and he mewls, his back arching. He's still lying mostly on his stomach but I've decided this is exactly how I want to take him.

"I'm gonna fuck you awake, beautiful," I murmur in his ear as I lean over him and grip his hair, tugging on it. He moans and damn, that's hot. "I'm gonna own this pretty hole," I continue, and with each word his cock gets harder and more precum leaks out onto the sheets. I slide my finger from his hole and grip his cock again.

He gasps and bends his knee, thrusting into my hand, chasing his pleasure, his eyes still closed. "Feel good, baby?" I ask, my voice low and husky as I stroke him.

"Yes," he whines. "God, yes, Hunter. Please don't stop. It feels so bloody good. Need you." I move away long enough to slide on a condom and slick my cock up with lube, him whimpering the entire time. He moves to his hands and knees, but I shove him back down so that he's flat on his stomach, his hard cock nestled between his body and the bed.

"I want you like this," I tell him. "You won't be moving at all, baby. You understand? I'm gonna do everything, just like yesterday. And just like yesterday, you're just going to lay there and take it, like a good boy." He shivers and nods.

I spread his cheeks and line my cock up with his entrance. In this position, his ass cheeks cocoon my cock, and it's hot as hell. I rub his lower back as my cock jerks, aching to be inside him. Then I shove forward, one hand on his hip and the other on his lower back. He whimpers as I let out a breath. Fuck, he's so hot and tight around me, and it feels so damn good, my cock is throbbing already.

"Shh," I soothe, continuing to rub his back. "You're doing so well, baby. So perfect for me. Your ass is taking my cock so beautifully." He starts to stroke himself but I remove my hand from his back and smack his. "No touching," I say. "Hands up by your head. Grip the pillow if you need to."

He whimpers but does as I say. "So good for me," I praise again, my hand returning to his lower back. I slide out, then push back in, this time not stopping until I'm fully sheathed in his incredible body, my balls resting against his ass. "Oh, fuck," I gasp. "Fuck, that's incredible. You feel amazing, baby."

His body trembles but he doesn't move other than that. I'm straddling him from behind now, his thighs underneath my ass, his hole clenching like a vice around my cock.

I rub his lower back again and press kisses to his shoulders. "Such a good boy," I purr, and another whimper escapes him. I can tell it's killing him not to move, but he is doing so well.

"I'm gonna fuck you so good, beautiful, you won't have a doubt in your mind who owns you," I tell him, as I start to move inside him. "You're gonna make me come so hard, baby."

"Nggg," he moans as I rest my hands on the mattress on either side of him and thrust my hips, pegging his sweet spot again and again. "You don't come until I say," I command. He nods.

"Did you fuck her last night, Oli?" I ask, and his eyes dart back to me. I keep thrusting and he nods. I growl.

"Did you come inside her?" I ask, and my thrusting gets harder and deeper when he nods again.

I grip his hair and he gasps as I pull on it. "Did you do as you were told and think of me?" He tries to nod again but can't with the grip I have on his hair. "Use your words," I demand.

"Yes," he gasps. "I thought of you. Only you."

I growl as I snap my hips harder and he shudders. God he feels so good. Love that I'm riding him, fucking him senseless and he's just taking it. I'm so fucking close. I release his hair and reach around to grab his cock again. He jerks and I moan at how goddamn hard he is, the sheet underneath him slick with precum.

"Goddamn, Oli," I growl. "You're so fucking hard for me, aren't you?" He nods on a whimper. "I'm gonna fuck you so hard you forget you ever let this cock anywhere near a pussy. Got it?" He nods again.

"Who's cock is this, Oli?" I ask, stroking him faster as I pound into him now with a relentless need. A need to fuck her and any thoughts of her right out of him. I need to fill him, use him, make him mine.

"Yours. Fuck, it's all yours, Hunter."

"It is, isn't it? It's mine, Oli, not hers, not yours. Mine. Only mine."

He nods furiously. "Christ, Hunter, please let me come."

I lean over and kiss his shoulder as I thrust again and again, feeling that tell tale ache in my balls as they draw up and my spine tingles. I come on a shout, my head thrown back, my cock pulsing as load after load of my release spills inside him.

"Please," he whimpers. I slide out of him slowly and grip his ass cheeks in my hands, burying my face in them, kissing them, nuzzling them, breathing in the scent of gingerbread, vanilla, sweat, and sex, then slipping off the condom and dribbling my cum out of it and along his ass cheeks until they're coated in me, before licking it off again, his mewls and whimpers music to my ears.

"Fuck," he moans, turning his head to look back at me. "Fuck, that's hot."

"Mmmm," I murmur in ascent. "Would you like to come

for me, Oli?" He nods vigorously and I grin, climbing off the bed and moving to sit in the chair a few feet away.

"Rub yourself off on the sheets, then," I tell him. "No hands. Just your big, beautiful cock on those fancy as hell sheets."

He grips the pillow and thrusts, his hips and ass muscles clenching, tightening, as he moves, his cock sliding along the silky white sheets until I see him trembling, gripping the pillow so tight his knuckles are white, his face flushed and sweat beaded on his brow.

"Stop," I demand, and he does, looking over at me with wide eyes. "Don't come."

"Fuck," he nearly growls. "You fucking bastard."

I grin. "I told you you would hurt for me, Oli," I remind him. "Again."

He blinks and his eyes widen again when he realizes what I'm up to. "Fuck you," he growls, and my grin widens further.

"Again," I repeat. He thrusts his hips against the sheets, his cock brushing against it, the tip red and angry, oozing precum. I let him go until he's shaking again. "Stop."

He nearly snarls at me. "You bloody wanker. How many times are you going to make me do this?"

"Again," I say. His face flushes and I see his jaw tick but he obeys, making my own cock spring back to life. Watching him rub off on the sheets is insanely erotic, especially knowing he won't come unless I give him the okay. His ass muscles clench again and again as he moves and his thighs tremble. "Slower," I tell him, and he adjusts his pace, his biceps bulging as he takes in a breath, gripping the pillow tighter.

It's not long before he speaks, and his voice is a pathetic whimper. "Please," he begs. "Please, I need to come." He turns to look at me and my cock jerks at the sight of tears sliding down his cheeks. Fuck, that's hot.

"I didn't tell you to stop," I reply once his hips cease their movement. He whimpers and keeps going, his cock straining and leaking like crazy. I let him move for a moment more, his body shaking, before I say, "come for me, baby." He lets out a choked sob, and a bellow leaves his throat as his cock shoots ropes of come onto the bed. My mouth salivates at the sight and I grip my now rock hard cock and jerk myself until I'm spraying a second time.

He collapses, a panting, gasping mess, his entire body beaded with sweat and flushed as he blinks away tears. I stand and move to him, pressing kisses to his back, before I grip his hair again and tug, forcing him to look at me. "Kiss me," I demand, and he rotates so that he's sitting on the bed, before I straddle him, and his lips lock with mine, my hand still gripping his sweat slicked, messy as fuck hair.

"You're a fucking devil," he murmurs, his body trembling still. I grin against his lips.

"You love it," I reply, and he hums, brushing his nose against mine.

"I do," he admits. "I really do."

"Fuck, Oli, you make me so hard," I tell him. "The way you surrender to me. It's so fucking hot. I've always enjoyed being in control in bed, but it's even better with you."

He grins and pecks my lips. "Happy to oblige."

"I think we should have a safeword. In case I ever go too far or ask you to do something you don't like." I stroke my fingers through his hair and he nods.

"All right. I'm not super well versed in kink but I believe red is the standard, yes?" I nod. "Red it is, then. And yellow to slow down." I nod again, and then kiss him once more.

$$\mathcal{S}\text{EVEN}$$

OLIVER

An hour later we're showered and packed, and on the road. Hunter is behind the wheel of the RV, and looking one hundred percent comfortable in jeans and a T-shirt, his beautiful blond hair up in a messy bun. I've decided I'm rather fond of his hair that way, though I like it no matter what.

The RV's not huge, but it's got more than enough space for the two of us, with a fold down queen sized sofa bed as well as a separate room with a queen sized bed, a television, full kitchen, and bathroom. The kitchen supplies and all the hookup accessories are included in the rental. That's what Hunter tells me, anyway. I haven't got the faintest clue what the hookup accessories are. I've never been in an RV in my life and my parents would probably be appalled at the idea of vacationing this way, but I find myself loving it the longer we're on the road. Hunter did have to spend a moment convincing me that it had in fact been cleaned and the sheets in particular were safe to sleep in. When he offered to stop somewhere and purchase a set of new sheets just to put my mind at ease I flushed and my chest constricted at his kindness. He didn't complain, didn't tell me I was being ridiculous, just did what he could to make sure I was comfortable.

Now I'm sitting next to him in the passenger seat as we make our way along the interstate. It's freeing to me, and I enjoy just sitting back and relaxing as Hunter drives, watching the landscape through the window. "Where are we headed?" I ask.

"We've got about an hour before we get to Cracker Barrel and then another four-ish hours before we reach Philly."

I frown. "What's a Cracker Barrel?"

He gapes at me, as if trying to suss out if I'm taking the piss or not.

"Are you serious?" he says, a note of laughter in his voice. "You've never been to a Cracker Barrel?"

I shake my head. "I've never been on a bloody road trip."

His eyes widen even further. "You're joking?"

"I joke not," I say. "You are witness to my first ever road trip."

"What did you do for family vacations growing up?"

"I don't know. Cruises, five star resorts. One year we came here, to the US. Of course, Olivia and I spent those vacations with the nanny so Mother and Father could enjoy themselves doing adult activities." I put the words in finger quotes. "That's how we came to live here, in fact. We visited New York and Mother fell so in love with it she insisted we move here. So we did."

He glances at me again. "Do you miss London?"

My chest squeezes again at his thoughtfulness. I don't know if anyone has ever asked me that before, even Amanda. "Sometimes," I say. "I would love to go back some day, but it seems I can never find the time, or someone to take there with me." I almost say I suggested it as an idea for our honeymoon before I realize that would be in poor taste. He doesn't need to think about that. Anyway, Amanda had her heart set on Hawaii, so there was no point in bringing it up.

"Well, you're in for a treat when we get to Cracker Barrel," he says. "It's this quaint country restaurant, and it's even got a little store inside with all these cool toys and candy and decorations you can't find anywhere else. And the food is amazing."

"It sounds lovely," I tell him, and he smiles at me.

HUNTER

Oliver is absolutely adorable when we reach Cracker Barrel, and is gazing at everything in the small shop with wide eyes like a child in a candy store, moving from rack to rack, picking things up, turning them around, pushing the buttons on the toys just to see what they'll do. Reading all the quotes on the decor, sometimes laughing and other times looking at me for help because he doesn't understand the joke. He loves the giant checkers board, a rug in place of an actual board, and I can tell he wants to play, so I sit in one of the oversized rocking chairs on one side and gesture for him to take the other. We don't finish the game before our name gets called. I can tell Oliver is disappointed, and I have to drag him along, reminding him that everything will still be there when we're finished, and he can come back.

His eyes roam as we make our way to our seats, taking in the unique decor on the walls, from vintage signs, to cast iron pots and pans, and farming equipment.

He flushes when he walks right into me, after I stop by the two person table the hostess has led us to. "Apologies," he says, and I just chuckle, taking my seat as he takes his.

The waitress comes by almost immediately to ask what we'd like to drink, and I order coffee. Oliver gets water. I have a feeling he'd get hot tea if they had it, but they don't. She scurries off when we tell her we need a minute to look over the menu. I don't really, since I've been here a million times, but I know Oliver does. God, he's adorable, his eyes darting around as he takes everything in. It's just a restaurant, but he seems quite taken with it, and it makes me happy. Giving him experiences like this warms my heart. There's nothing I want more than his happiness.

"You like it?" I ask.

He flushes again and smiles. "It's charming."

I almost reach across to squeeze his hand but then stop myself. I don't know if he is comfortable with me showing him affection in public. He's still coming to terms with his sexuality and I don't want to make him uncomfortable. God, it's hard not to touch him, though.

"What are you getting?" he inquires as he puruses the menu.

"Well, normally I would get a burger," I say, "but this new Fresh Berry French Toast Bake is calling my name." I lick my lips and he chuckles.

"It does look delicious," he says. "God, it must have a million calories."

"That's what vacations are for. Especially road trips."

"Eating unhealthy food?" he asks, eyeing me. I laugh.

"Yeah, it's like a rite of passage. Besides, we'll have plenty of healthy meals on the road, too. We brought plenty of food to cook."

He squirms like he's trying to convince himself it's okay to eat an unhealthy meal once in a while, and I don't know if it's adorable or sad. "Come on, Oli," I encourage, playfully. "Eat the French Toast. Join the Dark Side."

He smirks at me and I laugh. "You know you want to," I tease. "We can be bloated together."

"Christ, all right," he murmurs. "Anything to get you to shut the hell up."

I laugh as his eyes twinkle with amusement. The waitress returns with our drinks and we order our food. When she leaves again I grab the wooden triangle next to me with orange and yellow pegs slotted into the holes on top, and shove it towards the center of the table.

"What's this?" he asks.

"It's a game. You have to jump the pegs and try to leave as few left as possible. Wanna try?"

He does, and there's four left when he's finished. "Not bad for a first timer," I say, and he purses his lips.

"You can do better?"

"Watch and learn," I say. When I'm finished and there's only two left, he narrows his eyes at me. "What?"

"You cheated."

I laugh. "I did not cheat. You can't cheat at this game." His eyes are twinkling again and I shake my head. He tries again and does a little better, with only three left this time. He keeps trying until our food arrives and I decide I should take a photo. My stomach knots when I think about sending it to Mom like I promised. Less due to guilt over Oliver and I and more because, honestly, I don't want to share this with anyone. This moment, with him, us. I want to keep it for myself and lock it away safely, along with all the other things I'm learning about him.

"Ahh, yes!" he shouts, pumping his fist in the air and making the other patrons nearby turn their heads in our direction. I laugh and cover my mouth, and he flushes again as he apologies to no one in particular. "I did it," he says in a much softer tone, gesturing to the game and the two pegs remaining, beaming at me.

"And I'm very proud," I tell him, wishing more than anything I could kiss him right now.

Eight

HUNTER

After our meals, we return to the shop to pay for our food (the French Toast was absolutely worth the calories by the way) and to browse a bit more. I purchase a pecan log that I tell Oliver is delicious. A mixture of nougat, caramel, and of course, pecans.

Oliver is enraptured by a toy parrot that repeats what you say, moving its beak and wings as it does. I cave and purchase it for him when he isn't looking. We have batteries in the RV so we don't need those, and even though it's clearly a child's toy, I have a feeling he never really had much of a childhood, and it makes me happy to see him enjoying something so simple.

We use the bathroom and then climb back into the RV and head towards Philadelphia. I think one of my favorite things about being on this trip with Oliver is how dressed down he is. I've seen him in sweats a couple of times but never jeans or shorts, and he looks sexy as hell in both. His hair is less styled to perfection than usual, and I love the rumpled look on him. Makes it look like he just got fucked.

As I drive, I look over and see him pressing buttons on his

kindle. I didn't even know he had a kindle, or enjoyed reading.

"What are you reading?" I ask.

"Oh, nothing right now. I can't find anything that is keeping my attention unforuntately."

He sounds utterly morose, his bottom lip jutting out slightly in a pout that I don't think he even realizes he's doing, but it's adorable. "What do you like?"

He shrugs. "Fiction, mysteries, suspense, really anything with a good plot and decent characters that will let me escape for a bit."

"You read any romance?"

His cheeks pinken again and I can't help smiling when he clears his throat. "Not very much, no, I couldn't get into reading about straight sex, believe it or not. I tried it when I thought…" he trails off for a second. "When I thought it might help me…" he trails off again and I nod. God, did he make himself read straight romance or watch straight porn to try and convince himself he wasn't gay? Or to try and make himself not gay? I hate that he felt so ashamed and wanted to be anything other than who he is.

"There's gay romance, you know," I tell him. His eyes light up at that, and fuck, I can't even with this man.

"Really?"

"Yeah," I say, with a chuckle and a smile. "Tons of them, and they're really good."

"I wouldn't even know where to start."

"I can tell you some I like, if you want."

"You read gay romance?" he asks, seeming rather stunned at the idea.

"Yeah, I've gotten some great stuff for my spank bank from reading gay romance, plus lots of amazing stories, too. I love reading about characters I can relate to."

"Okay, tell me what to read," he says, finger poised over his kindle.

"Um, okay, well, it depends what you like."

He frowns and it's too fucking cute. Damn I need to feel his lips on mine. It's been too fucking long. "I don't know what I like."

"Okay, well, like there's different genres, like contemporary, fantasy, paranormal, historical. Then there's different tropes within the genre like, do you want a dark romance, or something angsty that might make you cry, or are you into the more feel good, fluffy stuff. There's friends to lovers, enemies to lovers, age gaps, second chance, single father, cowboys.There's even some taboo books that are really good if you're into that kind of thing."

He furrows his eyebrows. "Taboo? Like what?"

"Like stepbrothers, or blood relations if you want really taboo."

His eyes widen. "People write about blood relatives doing the hanky panky?"

I can't help laughing. "Yes. It's fiction." He nods.

"I don't think I'm ready for that quite yet, but stepbrothers sounds intriguing. Or friends to lovers, maybe. Or age gap." He flushes at that and I feel my cheeks heating slightly, too.

"Okay, well, if you want a good age gap you should try Until You by Felicity Snow. It's got some kink but I think you'll like it. If I'm wrong you can tell me. If you like that one she has a kinky stepbrother erotica you can try."

He nods and taps away at his kindle, then turns to show me the cover of a sexy silver fox running his fingers through his hair and the title, *Until You* displayed on the front along with the author's name. I nod. "That's it."

"Mmmm, I like it already," he practically purrs, and I laugh. I don't think I've ever heard him say something like that before, acknowledging his attraction to another man, real or otherwise, except me, of course.

He sits back in his seat and even puts his bare feet up on the dashboard as he reads, and I can't stop smiling. I've never seen him so relaxed.

Only five minutes later I'm pulling off the road and into a

rest stop, putting the RV in park. He looks up. "Is everything all right? Why did we stop?"

I'm unbuckled and out of my seat in an instant, gripping his face and pressing my lips to his. He grunts and drops his kindle, then moans when I grip his hair and tug. God, I love that. I tilt his head back, sliding my tongue in his mouth and hearing him whimper. My cock jerks and I climb into his lap, straddling him.

"Fuck," I breathe, when we've parted. His hair is a mess, his lips are swollen and covered in my spit and his eyes are blown wide. I can see his very hard cock tenting his shorts, and mine is throbbing too.

"Bloody hell. Did you pull over just to kiss me?"

"Maybe," I say. "You were just so fucking cute at the restaraunt and then having this conversation about steamy gay romance and…God, everything about you turns me on, Oli."

His eyes lock with mine for a second before he's gripping my hair and crashing our mouths back together, sucking and biting my lips. I unzip his pants in a frenzy and he does the same to me. We start to jack each other off and suck on each other's tongues at the same time, moaning and whimpering as we do. My cock throbs in his grip and he strokes me fast and hard.

"Fuck, Oli," I gasp. His hand feels so incredible around my cock, and the feel of his cock in my hand just adds to the desire I feel for him. I want to make him come so badly. I match his rhythm as I stroke him and capture his mouth with mine again. Seconds later he's whimpering into my mouth as I pick up my speed, gripping him harder, and I know he's close.

He comes hard only seconds later, whimpering into my mouth repeatedly as he does, his cock spasming in my grip as he shoots his release all over my hand and his shirt.

"Fuck," I cry. I'm so damn close. "Fuck, Oli." He grips my neck and bites down hard, and I cry out, my release coating his hand and dripping onto my lap. I lean forward and rest my forehead against his as I come down from the high of my orgasm.

"Was that okay?" he asks, gripping my hips, his hand still sticky with my release.

I nod. "Fuck, yes. That was hot as hell." He grins and pecks my lips again. Then we get cleaned up and head back out on the road.

OLIVER

It's nearly three in the afternoon by the time we reach Philadelphia. I've been enjoying my book so much I don't want to put it down, but I won't let Hunter handle everything. Once we've arrived at the campground he parks the RV and gets everything hooked up, while I watch so I know how to do it in the future. He makes it look easy, even backing the RV into our spot, when I'm sure it was anything but.

There's a lovely lake in front of us and lush greenery on all sides, giving us ample shade. We have a picnic table and our own grill. Birds fly overhead, and ducks sit on the sparkling clear blue water. There's a dock leading out over the lake and canoes and paddle boats for rental. There's also hiking trails nearby. Though honestly I'm perfectly content to just sit here and relax for now.

When everything is set up, we break out a blanket and chairs and arrange them outside the RV. I'm sitting on my chair, once again with my kindle, when Hunter emerges from the RV with a mug and hands it to me.

"What's this?" I say, setting my kindle on my lap and taking it. I inhale the scent of lemon and chamomile and relax as I breathe it in.

"You didn't get your tea earlier. I thought you might like some," he says, as he takes his place on the blanket near my feet and lies down, his hands behind his head and sunglasses on his face.

"Oh," I reply. "I wasn't even aware we brought the kettle."

I take a sip and it's utterly perfect, the right amount of milk and honey.

He shrugs. "I know you have tea every morning. I didn't want you going without. There's a few different flavors of tea bags in there. I just picked the one that sounded good."

I'm not sure what to say to that. He's right of course, but I never knew he noticed. "Thank you." I sip my tea and let it seep into my bones. I hardly need the warmth out here, with the sun beating down overhead, but I enjoy the taste and it's always been a pick me up. There's a nice breeze going at least, which makes the heat not as miserable. It's actually rather pleasant. I honestly can't remember the last time I just sat outside. The last time I relaxed before this trip, or I didn't have work or family or my own internal angst weighing me down. But here, I feel like I can be me; like I don't have to pretend or hide anything. Being with Hunter makes it easier for me to embrace the parts of myself I've kept buried for so long. Being on this trip with him is everything.

"So what's the plan for tomorrow?" I ask, taking another sip of my tea, and realize when he hums slightly that he was drifting to sleep. "Sorry, did I wake you?"

He shakes his head, and rubs my bare foot, and it's oddly sweet. "No, I thought we'd maybe visit the zoo, or an art museum or something? We'll have time for a few things. I like to stick to one activity a day and then spend the rest of the time relaxing."

"Sounds perfect to me." There's a pause before I find myself saying, "Fancy a swim? Then I'll make you supper."

"You're going to cook for me?" he asks, sitting up.

"Of course. I don't mind it, and you did all the driving."

He smiles. "Well, I won't say no."

We head into the RV to change and I gape when I see the bright blue speedo that Hunter slips into. It looks divine on him, all that gorgeous warm beige skin on display, and hugging his cock and balls so perfectly I almost whimper.

"Christ, you fucking tease," I murmur, and he gives a

wicked grin. "I'm going to have an epic boner the entire bloody time if you wear that."

"I have an extra," he says, pulling a red one out of his bag and holding it up for me, his eyes gleaming with mischief.

"Oh, God, no, I couldn't. No one wants to see these white legs and freckles. They'd go blind."

"You're joking." He moves closer to me and slides his hand along my thigh, making me gasp. "These are the sexiest fucking legs I've ever seen," he rumbles. He nibbles on my neck as he pops the button on my shorts and slides the zipper down over my hard on. "I would love to see you showing off this gorgeous body." He presses kisses to my neck and jaw and I shiver, then gasp as he tugs and my shorts fall to the floor, pooling at my feet.

"Christ, you little minx, you know I can't say no to you," I respond, my voice low. I can feel him grinning against my cheek before he grips the waistband of my underwear and slides them down, letting them fall on top of my shorts.

"Pick up your foot and hold on to me," he says, and I do. I bloody do whatever he tells me to do because I fucking love it. I love his bossiness and his bravado. I love his domination and control. I fucking crave it in a way I have never craved anything before. I love being given orders by him. I love not having to think about anything other than obeying him and knowing it will make him happy. Knowing it will make me happy.

I grip his shoulders and lift one foot, letting him slide the speedo on. "Good boy," he praises, and God, why does that have the effect on me that it does? Why do I melt and become so hard in an instant when he tells me I'm good? Why do I crave it so much when he gives me any type of praise? It just makes me want to please him more. It makes some of the self-hatred I've carried for so long not feel quite so heavy. Makes me feel a little more worthy, a little more loveable, each and every time.

"Other foot," he instructs and I do the same, shifting my

weight so he can slide the other end on me. Then I'm standing there while he slides it up and over my erection that has only gotten harder. I gasp when he sinks to his knees in front of me and my cock jerks as he presses kisses to my feet, then works his way up my legs, kissing my ankles, then my knees, then my thighs, before he presses a kiss to my balls, and then the tip of my cock. Christ, what is he trying to do to me? I can't stand the level of his affection, his care. The way he seems to know exactly what I need and when. I suck in a breath as my cock twitches. I'm honestly surprised when he doesn't pay more attention to my cock but I'm not disappointed. This is another level of intimacy, of respect, of worship, that I've never experienced. Fuck, I have tears filling my eyes as he makes his way up my torso, leaving more soft kisses in his wake, my body trembling. My face is flushed when he reaches my lips and kisses me.

"You're beautiful," he whispers against my lips. "Inside and out, Oli. Don't let anyone tell you otherwise."

I have no words, so I simply nod. Then we grab our towels and sunscreen and head back outside.

We spend quite a bit of time in the water before we lie on the grass on our towels, letting the sun dry us. I've become more comfortable in my swimwear after seeing Hunter's gaze on me multiple times and the way his body responds. It's flattering and a definite confidence booster. I think I actually like the speedo more than my regular swim trunks. It's quite comfortable, to be honest, and less constricting all around.

As we lay there in silence, enjoying the breeze and the sounds of nature, I feel Hunter sliding his hand into mine. It seems hesitant, though, a bit unsure.

"This okay?" he asks, turning to look at me. I squeeze his hand.

"Yes," I reply. "Why wouldn't it be?"

He shrugs. "I wasn't sure how you would feel about holding hands in public."

Oh, sweet boy. That he's thinking of me and wanting to

make sure I'm comfortable and safe is so utterly endearing. "Can I kiss you?" I ask, and he leans into me, our lips brushing. His lips are warm and soft and utterly perfect. The way he grips my neck, tangling his fingers in the hair there, the way he moves his lips over mine, the soft caresses, sliding his tongue inside to taste me every now and again, it's like nothing I've ever known before. His kisses are sensual, addicting. He kisses me like I deserve to be kissed, to be appreciated, to be savored. I've never had a kiss make me feel safe and worshiped at the same time, until him.

We kiss a while longer, before I sigh and run my fingers through his wet hair. "Why don't we go shower and change?" I suggest. "Then I'll make dinner." He nods and we head back inside.

Nine

HUNTER

Unfortunately the shower in the RV isn't even close to big enough for both of us, so I let Oliver go first and then shower while he works on supper. It starts raining shortly after I step out and towel off, and I love it. I've always found rain to be soothing, and curling up with a meal, a good book, or a tv show while it's coming down outside is one of my favorite ways to relax. That or a good nap. The pitter patter of the rain always seems to lull me to sleep.

I can't help but be slightly disappointed when Oliver is no longer wearing his speedo. He looked so fucking sexy in it and I can't wait to get it on him again. He is looking awfully cozy and adorable in the sweats and T-shirt he's wearing now, though. He's slipping on oven mitts and opening the oven door when I come out of the small bathroom, and his gaze catches on me as I wander through the RV naked, in search of my clothes.

"Jesus, you're going to cause a permanent injury if you keep that up," he grouses.

"I'm fine," I reply.

"I meant me," he says. "I can't focus on not burning myself while you're…like that."

I laugh as I slide my briefs on, then slip into a T-shirt and sweats as well. "I'm sorry, I'll be more considerate next time," I say, sliding up next to him as he closes the oven door and slips the oven mitts off. I press a kiss to his neck as he sets the timer, and he squirms.

"What's for dinner?" I ask, slipping my arms around his waist and continuing to press kisses to his soft skin. God, he smells good.

He shivers against me. "I'm sorry, did you say something?" he says after a moment.

I chuckle again. "Dinner, baby, what's for dinner?"

He moans softly as my hand slips under the front of his shirt and rests on his abdomen, fingers playing with the happy trail there, my lips brushing against his ear. I can see his cock thickening and beginning to tent his sweats.

"Food," he replies, the word breathy, and I laugh softly.

"I have an idea of what we can do while we wait," I murmur.

"Fuck." He gasps as my fingers slip under the waistband of his briefs and his cock jerks. Some of his precum lands on my fingers and I use it to tease him, sliding my fingers along his shaft but not gripping. He moans and thrusts his hips, seaking friction. "Want something, beautiful?" I ask.

"Christ, you're such a bellend," he grouses. "Just bloody touch me."

I laugh and then step back, my hand slipping out of his briefs, before I kneel behind him. "Hands on the counter, baby. I'm gonna eat you out until you're begging to come."

"Oh, fuck," he gasps as I pull his sweats down, and then slowly, slowly, kiss my way down his ass cheeks as I lower his underwear, before sliding them down his thighs and letting them fall to the floor as his legs quake. I grip his thighs and massage them before moving my hands up to his ass cheeks and continuing my ministrations, burying my nose in his crack and inhaling. I moan at the smell of him—gingerbread, vanilla, and sunshine.

"Christ," he breathes.

"Mmmm," I hum, drunk off his scent and the feel of soft skin against my face and hands. "God, Oli, I could touch you forever."

He trembles at my words and it's fucking delicious. I nibble a couple more times on his ass cheeks, kneading them in my hands before I spread his cheeks and slide my tongue over his taint. He bucks and cries out, and I have to grip him and hold him in place. "Stay still, baby," I tell him gently. "Make all the fucking noises you want, but don't move. Understand?"

He nods and I spread his cheeks again as I feel his body tensing, his grip on the counter tightening, no doubt. I lick up his taint and over his hole again, savoring the sensation of his perfect bud fluttering against my tongue. "So fucking eager," I murmur, then make another pass. "So fucking ready to be filled." Another swipe of my tongue, slow and languid. "To be used. You want that, Oli?" Another pass. "You want to be fucked with my tongue, baby? Want it buried inside you? Want me to make you feel good?"

"Shit," he whimpers, his body trembling as his hole flutters incessantly. I hear the way his next word leaves, on a broken plea, and I can tell he's crying. "Please."

"Good boy," I say, and I hear his muffled sobs. "Shh," I soothe. "You're doing so well for me, Oli. You're gonna come so hard for me, aren't you, sweetheart?" He nods. "Since I can't speak while I'm inside you I'll tap your thigh to give you permission to come." He nods again, and I spread his cheeks once more, this time sliding my tongue over his pucker and then slipping it inside his hole. I feel his body spasming around me as I move my tongue inside him, hearing his whimpers and cries of pleasure as I eat him out.

"Oh, God, Oh, God, Oh, God. Fuck, Hunter, please," he begs, and I soar. "Please let me come."

I moan and tap his thigh, and seconds later I feel his ass clenching around my tongue, his thighs quaking, as his orgasm crashes into him.

"Oh fuck," he breathes as my tongue slides out, and I see the spunk painting the cupboards in front of him, his hands still gripping the counter top. Fuck, he came untouched with just my tongue inside him. Damn, that's hot. I grip him and move him aside gently before I slide my tongue over the mess he made that's trickling down the cupboard and onto the floor, before swallowing it down.

"Holy hell," he rasps. "I can't decide if that's insanely hot or insanely disgusting."

"I can't decide if that's insanely hot or insanely disgusting," a mechanical voice echoes, and I start cracking up as Oliver's eyes widen.

"What the bloody hell was that?" he asks, sliding his briefs and pants back up in a rush, his face flaming as the voice repeats his words a second time.

I'm still laughing as he makes his way through the RV searching for an intruder. He returns with the talking parrot in his arms and a grin on his face. "You bought this?" he says.

"You bought this?" the bird echoes again.

"Oh, bloody hell," Oliver grumbles as he turns the bird over to switch it off and we hear the first part of "Oh, bloody —" before he succeeds.

"You liked it," I say with a smile and a shrug. "Making you happy doesn't just involve my body."

He kneels next to me, as I haven't bothered to get up yet, and presses a kiss to my lips. "You, Hunter Price, are remarkable," he tells me, and I smile against his lips. "Now how do we make sure this thing doesn't interrupt us post coitus anymore?"

I laugh. "You turned it off, it should be good."

"Bloody hell, that was terrifying," he says, running a hand through his hair.

"Funny as hell, though," I say, and he narrows his eyes at me.

"Yes, I'm sure it was delightful to watch me stumbling to dress and walk around like a lunatic all for the sake of a toy bird."

"I mean as far as entertainment goes I'd give it a solid eight out of ten."

"You little arse," he quips, his eyes twinkling as he reaches out and begins to tickle me. I shriek and roll onto my back, gasping when he doesn't let up. I'm laughing so hard I have tears sliding down my cheeks. But then he's pinning me underneath him and kissing me breathless.

OLIVER

The next morning we wake bright and early to get ready for our day at the zoo. We slept in each other's arms last night, and I honestly can't remember when I've felt more safe or at peace. Hunter's body pressed close to mine, his warm breath against my neck and his arms slung over me. I slept better than I've slept in years, and really didn't want to get out of bed. However, Hunter coaxed me up with the smell of tea, freshly baked rolls, and fresh fruit, so I can't complain too much.

We eat, then shower again and dress before packing a small backpack with some water bottles, sunscreen, and a couple of small snacks. Hunter ties his hair up in a messy bun again and puts a red baseball cap on, the messy bun sticking out of the back. It's honestly incredibly hot, especially since he's wearing shorts and one of those loose fitting muscle tanks with the oversized arm holes so you can bloody see his entire chest. Not that I'm complaining. I don't think I ever fully appreciated those shirts until now.

I slide my sunglasses on and we catch one of the buses that makes trips to and from the zoo, arriving shortly after they open.

"We should get a picture," Hunter says, "for Mom." We stop at the zoo entrance and take a selfie. Hunter sticks his tongue out and raises his fingers in a peace sign. I simply smile. Then he turns and surprises me by pressing his lips to my cheek and taking another photo, his hand gripping my neck in a way that feels almost possessive.

When he shows it to me I can't help smiling more. We look happy. "We won't be sending that one to Mom," he tells me, a note of melancholy in his voice and the sparkle in his eyes dimming a bit. But it doesn't last long before he's gripping my hand and pulling me towards the ticket counter.

We make our way around to all of the different animals, starting with the Golden Lion Tamarin, which I've never heard of before, but is a type of endangered monkey.

We see the llamas, the reptiles and amphibians, before making our way to the barnyard animals. Then we stop at the Primate Preserve to see the gorillas, monkeys, and lemurs.

Afterwards, we break for lunch. It's nothing fancy but it's decent and it fills me up, giving me enough energy to continue our afternoon, which I'm finding myself enjoying immensely. I can't remember the last time I was at a zoo, and I've always loved animals. I wanted a pet growing up but Mother and Father never allowed it; said it would be too much work. I'd thought of getting one as an adult but worried I wouldn't have the time to care for it properly with the hours I keep. Maybe that's something I should reconsider since I recently started working from home. I do get lonely, though not as much with Hunter around. My chest squeezes at the thought of him leaving at the end of the month.

After visiting Big Cat Falls we take a ride on the carousel. However, rather than horses, it's all different kinds of zoo animals. I'm a bit flustered at the idea as I consider carousels to be for children but Hunter grips my hand and pulls me along, assuring me it's perfectly fine, and I find myself smiling like an idiot the entire time as we ride next to each other, me on a panther and him on a giant tortoise.

"Christ, I don't think I've been on one of those since I was five and my nanny took Olivia and I to the fair," I tell Hunter once we've gotten off and started walking again.

"Really?"

I nod.

"Jesus, that's depressing."

"It was worse when she got scolded for taking us, bringing us home covered in dirt and cotton candy and smelling like barn animals. My parents were horrified, and even though Olivia and I loved it we never went back."

"What did they let you guys do?" he asks. "Did you even get to be kids?"

I chuckle slightly. "Oh, they had us signed up for so many lessons we stayed busy that way. Or they would ship us off to some high end summer camp somewhere. I took piano, which they made me practice religiously, and Olivia did dance. We both had swimming lessons, which I actually enjoyed for the most part, and Olivia took equestrian classes, too. I ended up being on the swim team in high school because that, tennis, and golf were the only sports they would allow. They also had us take etiquette classes. It wasn't terrible, but clearly not as enjoyable as a fair, and less for our benefit and more for theirs."

"You play piano?" he says. I nod.

"Are you any good?" He gives me a cheeky grin.

"Quite good, actually, though it's been a long time, so I'm rather rusty. I did win my share of competitions, though. Honestly, it was never something I did for myself, just another thing to be the good son they wanted me to be. They loved bragging to all their rich friends about how good I was, but I think that made me grow to resent it more. I got an earful when I started college and told them I was quitting."

"I bet," he says, then grips my hand again.

"Want some ice cream?" I nod and we indulge in some soft serve cones, trying to gobble them down before they melt all over us. Hunter reaches over and wipes some ice cream that has dribbled down my chin onto his thumb before putting it in his mouth and sucking it off, staring right at me the entire time. And yes, my cock twitches.

We wash our hands after, and reapply sunscreen since it's been a while, then continue on our way, passing the scads of different birds, before we reach Otter Falls, where we see the Giant River Otter, another endangered animal. Right next to the otters are two more endangered animals, the Rodrigues Fruit Bat and the Red Panda, which looks similar to a fox, in my opinion, with its white and red fur, and is quite cute. I'm finding out about so many animals I didn't even realize existed today and the wealth of knowledge is fascinating. Hunter snaps a few more pictures on his phone as I read about them. The Rodrigues Fruit Bat apparently lives in colonies consisting of one male and several females, much like a harem, which I point out to Hunter and he smirks. "Intrigued?" he says.

"Quite," I reply, smiling. "Doesn't seem so bad. Though I think I might do it a little differently." He chuckles and pecks my cheek.

"I can't believe you just said that."

Honestly, I can't either, but I find it liberating to talk about my sexuality and desires. Things I've never dared voice before, or even let take up much space in my head. Not that I actually want a harem of men, but, "Are there books like that?" I say, turning to him. "With male harems?"

He nods. "Sure are, and they're hot as hell."

I grin. "Ooh, I do think I would like reading that."

He chuckles and pulls me along.

We make our way to the African Plains where we pay to feed the giraffes, and Hunter cackles when the one I'm feeding leans down and licks my face, making me splutter. The attendants apologize and give me something to clean myself with, thankfully.

Next is the zebra and rhinoceros, followed by the penguins and bears.

By the time we've seen everything there is to see, I'm knackered, and Hunter looks pretty tired too. We head back to our campsite and collapse on the bed after stripping down to just our underwear, curled up in each other's arms once again.

I wake to a rock hard cock against my arse and moan when Hunter begins to rut against me, his hand on my hip in a death grip. "Fuck, Oli I need you," he breathes. "Need you so bad, baby. It's been too damn long since I've been inside you." I feel my underwear sliding down to just underneath my arse cheeks in the back, the air against my naked skin arousing me further, making my hole flutter and my cock twitch. I'm so damn hard already, my precum leaking through my underwear in the front where they're pulling tight against my erection.

I hear the tell tale sound of the cap on the lube bottle clicking open and bend my top leg, allowing him better access. "Fuck, you're perfect," he murmurs. "So fucking perfect for me, Oli. You gonna let me fuck you, baby? Gonna let me use this pretty hole until I'm coming inside you?" I nod, my cock throbbing now and oozing copious amounts of precum, a large wet spot forming on my underwear.

"Such a good boy," Hunter purrs as his cock lines up with my hole. "I'm gonna leave your underwear around your cock, baby. Wanna see how wet I can make you." Fuck, why is that so hot? My cock jerks repeatedly as he runs his finger up and down it. "You won't come this time," he says, his lips ghosting over my ear. "You'll let me use you, touch you, however I want, but you won't come. This is for me. My pleasure. Understand, beautiful?" I'm shaking when I nod. He reaches out and slaps my cock, making me gasp.

"Fuck," I cry.

"Use your words, Oli," he instructs. "Understand?"

"Yes," I answer, breathlessly.

"Yes, what?"

"I won't come. I'll let you use me, but I won't come."

"Good boy," he says again, then grips my hip again and pushes his cock inside me. It burns as he fills me, stretches me, uses me, having not been stretched first, but the more he fills me, the more the pain ebbs and pleasure takes over, until he's fully seated inside me and my cock is throbbing, aching to be touched, begging for release that I know I won't get. His arm wraps around me and he holds me to him, as he pulls out almost all the way and then shoves back in. He does it again, pulling out slightly less, before pushing all the way back inside. I hate that we have to have a barrier between us. I want his bare cock inside me so badly. Want him to fill me with his seed until I can't take anymore.

"God, that's good," he moans, sliding in and out of me slowly, using me, claiming me. He presses kisses to my shoulder and upper back, his leg slung over mine as he moves, impaling me on his cock. Every movement sends shockwaves of pleasure through my body, and my underwear is soaked in my precum, my cock so hard it hurts. "So damn good, Oli. You feel fucking amazing, baby, choking my cock. So tight, so hot. God, I want to stay inside you forever."

I whimper when his dick pegs my prostate over and over as he thrusts inside me, chasing his pleasure, then gasp when he grips my hair with his other hand and yanks, making my cock spasm. I'm so close to coming I can't stop the tears from sliding down my cheeks.

"You're doing so well for me, sweetheart," he praises, and I sob harder as my cock jerks. I don't think I've ever been so hard in my life, so desperate for release. "So good for me, sweet Oli. Your ass was made to take my cock, beautiful." His thrusts are torturous, just perfect enough that I'm being kept on the edge but unable to come.

"Gonna come now, baby," he tells me, picking up his pace. His grip on my hair tightens as does the arm around my middle. I'm terrified I'll come, but seconds later he's moaning, "Oh, God, Oli, fuck, so good, baby, so damn good," as he milks himself on my arse and I feel his warmth filling the condom buried deep inside me. He collapses against my back, his leg still slung over mine. He presses more kisses to my heated skin and slides out of me, my body trembling still as I breathe and try to convince my cock to calm down.

I hear him sliding off the condom. "Roll over," he tells me, and I do, my arse still bare and my cock still leaking profusely and straining against my briefs. "Fuck, that's hot," he says as he stares at my cock and the large wet spot it's created. He leans over and presses a kiss to the tip and I whimper. Then he's holding up the condom that I'd assumed he'd discarded and says, "open up, beautiful." I do and he positions the used condom over my mouth, and then tilts it, letting his spunk slide out, and onto my tongue.

"God, have mercy," he murmurs as he watches me, and I can't help the sense of pride that fills me. "Don't swallow yet."

I do as he says and let it gather on my tongue, holding my mouth open as the last bit slips inside. He tosses the condom and then climbs on top of me and licks inside my mouth, tasting himself on me, moaning as he does. Fuck, it's so damn filthy and so fucking erotic, my cock is ready to burst. "Now swallow," he says, and I do.

"God, Oli, the things you do to me." He runs his fingers through my hair as he stares down at me and I grip his hips. I thrust up into him and he smirks.

"Do you need something?"

I nod as I continue to gyrate.

"What do you need?" he says, the little prick. He bloody well knows what I need. He fucking did this to me.

"I need to come," I tell him, my voice raspy. "Please?"

He leans down and kisses me again, slow and languid. "Later," he says, pulling away. He scoots down and gazes at my very hard cock. Then tortures me by leaning down and licking a stripe up my shaft. "I like you like this, Oli. You're so pretty. So fucking hard for me. You're going to stay this way for a while." I squirm and shake my head, and he grips my hair again, pulling enough to make me stop. "I told you you would hurt for me, Oli, remember?" I feel tears filling my eyes again but nod. "Good boy," he says, and my heart leaps right along with my dick. "We're going to eat dinner first, and then go for a swim in the lake again. And maybe after that, if you're really good, I'll let you come, okay? But you're going to stay hard for me until then." My eyes widen and I open my mouth but he puts a finger to my lips. "Are you safewording, baby?"

I shake my head furiously even as my cock throbs. Fuck, he's a monster. He edged me yesterday for a few minutes and it was torture. This time it will be a few hours.

"What's your color?"

"Green," I squeak out.

He grins and kisses me again. "I want you to change into your speedo, and then you're going to wear it while I make us dinner and we eat. You will stroke yourself if you lose your erection, but you will not come. Understand?"

Jesus Christ. I nod, even as tears slide down my cheeks. He kisses me yet again and murmurs, "Good boy," against my lips.

He climbs off of me and moves out of the small bedroom to the main area of the RV while I slip out of my underwear and into my speedo. I'm big enough it barely contains me when I'm this hard, the tip of my cock almost peeking out at the top.

Hunter purrs when I enter the room, licking his lips. "Beautiful."

I flush and kiss him. "Can I help with dinner?"

He shakes his head and holds up the patties he pulled out of the refrigerator. "I'm going to go grill these. You can join me or stay inside. Just make sure you stay hard."

"I can't go out there like this," I retort. "God, I'll get arrested."

"Where's your sense of adventure?" he says, a twinkle in his eyes, then pecks my lips.

I pout, my bottom lip jutting out and my arms crossed over my chest. He grins and heads outside.

I last two minutes before I'm joining him, damn the consequences. If anyone happens to come by I'll hide myself or go back inside, but I don't want to be alone.

I try reading my book while I sit and wait for him to make the hamburgers but give up after only a few minutes. I huff as I set it aside.

"What's wrong?" he asks, looking back at me.

"I can't read my bloody book without getting even harder," I grouse, and he grins.

"You like it?"

"Yes, but I'd like it more if I could fucking come."

"Dinner's almost ready," he says. "And then we'll swim."

Christ it's taking everything in me not to hump the nearest goddamn tree, or rub up against Hunter and blow my load. This is bloody torture.

I have to stroke myself during dinner as my erection fades and Hunter watches me with an intensity that has my cheeks flushing and my cock twitching. Bloody hell.

"Damn you look good doing that," he mutters, his eyes wide with lust and his own cock tenting his shorts.

I can't deny the pleasure and satisfaction it gives me to know my body does that to him.

We finish our food and I wait for Hunter to change into his speedo, knowing that will be enough to keep me hard for a while without touching myself.

The water is wonderful. Cool, refreshing, and exactly what I needed after a long, hot day and being on my feet for several hours.

"Come on, jump in," he coaxes, standing on the edge of the dock as I tread water and shake my head ruefully.

"I'm far too old for that," I tell him. "And the last thing we need is a trip to the ER."

He laughs and then shouts as he leaps up, tucking his legs

under him, and makes a huge splash when he hits the water. Oh, to be twenty-one.

He's underwater long enough I start to worry, but then I'm shrieking as he pops up right underneath me, my legs over his shoulders as he dunks us both under again. When I come back up he's right there, gazing at me with an intensity I can't fathom. What does this beautiful boy see in me? Why does he crave me the way I crave him? When I look at Hunter I see everything I wish I could have been when I was younger. Wild, carefree, and happy. With him now I catch glimpses of those things, but know I can't hold on to them. Life will return to normal after this trip and things will go back to the status quo. I will be the man I've always been. The one who was only ever a sliver of his true self.

He makes me feel alive in a way I've never felt before. Makes me horny in a way I've never been before, and sees something in me I've never been able to see in myself.

Before I can even register it, he's sliding his hand behind my neck and pulling me to him, moving us a few feet closer to the bank so we can touch, the water still reaching our stomachs, before pressing his lips to mine. The wetness of our bodies against each other is intoxicating and I open my mouth, letting him inside as the sun begins its descent behind the trees, the yellow, orange and red hues stretching like a perfectly painted canvas across the sky.

His other hand slides around and slips inside my speedo, shoving the back down so my arse is exposed, the cool water kissing my bare skin and making me shiver. He grips my arse cheek as he kneads the flesh over and over, devouring me and making me so damn hard I can barely breathe. His cock is hard and slick and slides against mine as I kiss him back, my hands on his narrow hips, the feel of his wet skin electric against my palms.

"You've been hard this whole time," he says, resting his forehead against mine. I nod, feeling his breath ghost over my face. Every time I felt myself getting flaccid again I did as he instructed, even though he may not have even known. I wanted to do it. I wanted to please him. He kisses me again and I whimper when his hand moves from my arse to my cock, gripping me over my speedo and stroking me in such a delicious way that I find myself trembling and wrapping my arms around his neck for support.

"Christ, please don't tell me you're edging me again," I moan as his hand moves up and down my shaft again and again. My cock throbs at his touch, the feel of the wet nylon material against me producing a friction I can only describe as euphoric.

"Not this time, Oli," he whispers as he strokes me harder now, his voice almost reverent. "This time you're going to come for me, okay?" I nod my assent, our foreheads still pressed together, and whimper when he captures my lips with his again, continuing to stroke me through my speedo as his tongue delves inside, tasting me. I whimper again when I feel his hand moving from my cock and his finger sliding down my arse crack, before slipping inside me and making me gasp. He grips my hair hard again and I shiver as he presses me to him.

"Rub up against me while I fuck your ass, baby," he says. "You're gonna come so hard for me, Oli. You're gonna fill these speedos with your pretty spunk, aren't you, sweetheart?" His voice is a low growl and it sends a shiver straight to my cock.

I gasp again when his finger hits my sweet spot and I fucking hump him as I cling to him, my breath coming in harsh pants as he nudges my prostate again and again. His hard stomach gives me the perfect friction and my cock is aching as my fingers dig into his shoulders and upper back, my balls drawing up.

"Fuck, you're hot," he growls. "Keep using me, baby. Don't stop. Want you to come so fucking hard, Oli."

I thrust my hips forward relentlessly, and then press back

into his hand over and over, chasing my release. "Oh, God," I whine. "Fuck, Hunter, please, I can't..."

My words trail off and I'm a panting, gasping mess when he says, "Come for me, Oli. Say my name, baby. Scream for me."

"Hunter!" I cry, my head falling back as my arse clenches around his finger and my cock spurts load after load of my release into my speedo and onto his stomach. There's so much of it I even feel it sliding down my legs.

He strokes his fingers through my hair and presses kisses to my forehead as he slides his finger out of me and pulls my speedo back up over my arse. My eyes are closed as I shake with the aftershocks of my release.

"Beautiful," he whispers. "So fucking beautiful, Oli. Let's get cleaned up and I'll make you some tea, hmm?"

I nod and he takes my hand, helping me from the water. I shower, and when I get out, Hunter has my tea waiting. I take it and we head back outside, the sky giving way to dusk as the stars come out, the moon reflecting off the surface of the water, crickets and birds chirping, leaves rustling. An owl hoots in the distance, and I sigh in contentment as I take a sip of the earl gray tea.

Hunter lies down on the blanket and scrolls on his phone as I pick up my kindle and find my place in my book again. I'm absolutely loving the one he recommended. I feel like I can relate to Paul and his attraction to Charlie, fighting it even though he's absolutely taken by the younger, pretty boy. And I've never read a gay sex scene but I'm enjoying it very much. I have a feeling a whole new world has opened up to me. The thought of hiding my reading material from Amanda, though, is depressing, and I feel like that's just one more thing for me to feel guilt and shame over, rather than being able to embrace and enjoy it. I sigh, trying not to let that bother me now, while I'm here with Hunter.

I finish my tea and then move to lie next to him on the blanket. I lie with my head on his legs and he smiles down at me, then starts to stroke my hair as I read. "You enjoying it?" he asks.

"I am, " I tell him. "Thank you for giving me this. The book, yes, but just everything, really. Allowing me to discover who I am and creating a safe space for me to do so. I've never had that, and it means a lot, even if it can't last forever."

I can't make out his expression in the darkness but his fingers start to move a little differently through my hair. "No one should ever have made you feel like you had to disguise yourself, Oliver. There's nothing wrong with who you are. Your parents are blind to not see that." He pauses and I have a feeling he's not sure if he should say whatever is on his mind, but then I hear, "You're allowed to disappoint them, you know. You only get one life, Oli. Don't use it to make other people happy at the expense of your own happiness."

I know he means well, and he's probably right. But I've been living my life to please my parents for so long I don't know how to do differently. And part of me feels like chasing my own happiness is selfish. Maybe my parents want me to feel that way so they can control me. I don't know, I just know I've always felt like I wasn't good enough, and I keep reaching, trying, hoping, that one day I will be worthy of their love.

Ten

OLIVER

We sleep in the following morning and I wake to the smell of coffee and bacon. Of course, when I stumble out of bed, Hunter has the kettle simmering. There's croissants on the counter, and I spread some butter and jam on top of one and gobble it down in only a few bites. Hunter kisses me and slaps my arse before he pours himself some coffee. We eat and then shower before dressing and heading to the next stop on our adventure, the Reading Terminal Market. We have to walk a couple of blocks to the subway which stops nearby.

I've never heard of it, which doesn't surprise me, but I guess it's one of America's oldest and largest public markets, carrying all kinds of produce, meats, seafood, baked goods, cheeses and home decor. We're hoping to find something that we can turn into a delicious meal and also maybe a treat or two. Maybe even eat at one of the many restaurants on the premises of the historic building it's housed in.

There's so many different vendors that all sound amazing. I don't know how we'll get to all of them in one afternoon. Our first stop is a vendor that sells handcrafted African inspired jewelry and it's exquisite. I purchase some earrings for Amanda and try not to think too hard about whether the gesture is a result of affection, or guilt.

We stop at another vendor that sells honey, candles, and soaps that all look and smell incredible, and another that sells gorgeous linens. The entire place is filled to overflowing with shoppers browsing, and while I'm enjoying myself, I'm also feeling a bit anxious about losing my way in this large of a crowd in a place I've never been before. Moments later, Hunter's hand is in mine, giving it a gentle squeeze, and I relax. The freedom to hold his hand in public is one I don't take for granted, and I know I will miss it when we return home. Being here, where no one knows who we are, and I don't have the fear of being judged makes me squeeze his hand in return.

We continue on, and there's so many delicious looking treats at the multiple bakeries I know I will be leaving here with more sweets than I know what to do with. But Hunter will still encourage me to eat every single one.

We purchase fresh banana bread and several cookies before making our way to a vendor that sells fresh made, hand rolled donuts. When we hear it's only ten dollars for a dozen we give in and I just know I'll be gaining weight on this trip, but find myself caring less and less. Especially when I take my first bite and moan around it like a fucking porn star.

Hunter laughs. "Keep it PG, Oli," he teases, "there's children here."

"Piss off," I tease, then take another bite. "God, it's like having an orgasm in your mouth." He laughs again.

We've gotten the assorted variety and mine is the S'mores one, while Hunter has chosen one with fresh vanilla frosting and m&ms. We trade after that and sample each others' before switching back.

"Christ, they should warn you before you come here that

you'll leave having traded your wallet for an extra ten pounds."

Hunter's eyes twinkle as he grins at me, then licks some frosting off his bottom lip.

When we spot a stand that has gorgeous bouquets of flowers on display, Hunter tugs me over, and I smile when he leans over to smell an arrangement of peonies, sunflowers, and zinnias. There's also some lovely tulips, chrysanthemums, and roses, as well as lilies, and so many more.

"What do you like best?" he asks me, and I look around for a moment before pointing out a bouquet of sunflowers, ivy and small purple forget me nots.

"Excuse me," he says to the woman manning the shop, "I'll take those, please."

I'm flushing so deeply when he pays and then turns and hands me the bouquet that I must look like a tomato, but I can't wipe the smile from my face as I take them and breathe them in.

"Thank you," I say. I can't believe it but I can feel tears pricking at the corners of my eyes. "No one's ever bought me flowers before."

He kisses my cheek and then takes my hand again as we continue on our way. We stop at a place that sells fancy corndogs and decide that's where we'll have our lunch, before moving on. When we come upon a stand in the midst of the bustling market that sells tea, both in cups and in canisters that sit atop wooden shelves, we stop again. There's so many different flavors it's hard to narrow it down, but after being allowed to smell a few different ones, I decide on a ginger and peach blend that's delicious and we take a short break while I sip. When we find a coffee stand I insist on purchasing something for Hunter, and he chooses a cappuccino which he sips happily as we walk.

Lastly, we make a stop in the meat and poultry section and purchase a beautiful brisket to cook that evening.

We nap again when we return to the RV and then enjoy

the lake in the late afternoon before supper. We watch a movie while dining and then head outside and lie on our blanket again to gaze at the stars.

"I really enjoyed spending time with you today," Hunter says as we lie side by side, pointing out different conglomerations of stars and what we think they look like. Hunter doesn't hesitate to direct my attention to one that looks like a penis, making me laugh.

He presses a kiss to my cheek. "I really enjoyed being with you, too," I tell him, and he slides his hand around to grip my neck, nuzzling my nose with his before he kisses me.

The kisses grow more heated rather quickly and then he's climbing on top of me and I feel his hard cock pressing against mine as our tongues tangle. When he reaches down to stroke my cock, I moan and run my fingers through his hair. He presses kisses to my neck, then lifts the hem of my shirt and kisses his way from my belly button to my pecs, where he slides his tongue over my nipple, making me gasp, before he nibbles and sucks on the hard nub. He moves to the other nipple and repeats the gesture and I let out a string of undignified noises. When he grips my waistband and tugs, I don't hesitate in lifting my hips for him. There's nothing I want more right now than to let him take me under the stars, and there's no one else around, so why not?

He must have planned this, because he's got a packet of lube and condom ready as soon as his own shorts are off and lying next to mine. His body is breathtaking in the moonlight, his hard cock glistening as he coats it in lube. I bend my knees and spread my legs for him. He doesn't spend much time stretching me before he's at my hole and pressing inside. I grip his shoulders as my legs rest against his arms and he bottoms out, his eyes not leaving mine the entire time. And I can't help but feel like we're doing something other than just fucking; like I'm being made love to; like the way he touches me and kisses me and looks at me isn't just a desire to make me happy. He doesn't just want to make me feel owned and bring me pleasure. He wants me to feel cherished, valued, worthy, adored. And I'm floored by the knowledge that this man, this boy, has captured my heart so completely in such a short amount of time.

We come together, each other's name on our lips, and when I fall asleep in his arms that night, I can't help wishing we could stay this way forever. Because no matter how hard I try, I don't think I'll be able to keep myself from falling in love with Hunter Price.

HUNTER

"Christ, this is pure, unadulterated porn," Oliver remarks from his seat next to me. We're on the road again, on our way to Baltimore, but I have a surprise stop for Oli on the way there. He seemed a bit more morose last night and this morning and I'm hoping it will cheer him up.

I laugh. "*Until You?*"

He's so engrossed in his book he doesn't register that I asked him a question until several seconds later. "Hmm?" he says, lifting his head and looking at me.

I laugh again. "You still reading *Until You*? It was spicy but I wouldn't call it porn."

"Oh, no, I finished that a bit ago and just started *Stepbrother Mine* by the same author. Christ these two are filthy. Nothing but kinky sex for pages. Although I am enjoying the flashbacks. Those are sweet. And don't get me wrong, I'm enjoying the sex too, I just might need to change my underwear after."

I cackle. "It's pretty hot," I agree, and let him keep reading.

"It's pretty hot," we hear from behind us.

"What the hell?" I say, laughing. "I thought you turned it off."

"I did," Oliver grouses, slipping out of his seat and searching for the mechanical bird. It hasn't mimicked us in a while and now it's going at it again. A moment later he's bringing it back to his seat and sitting down with it as he examines it. "It's on again. How did that happen?"

I shrug. "Beats the hell out of me. I think it might be possessed."

He turns it off again as it starts to repeat my words and sets it aside. "Can we find another one?" he asks, and I start, looking at him.

"You want another talking bird?" His eyes widen so much it's comical.

"Oh, dear God, no, I meant the restaurant. Barrel whatever?" I laugh again.

"Cracker Barrel," I say, and he nods.

"Yeah, I'm sure we can find one on the way." He grins and we sit in silence for a moment longer before he speaks again.

"You're majoring in psychology, correct?"

I glance at him. "Yeah, why?"

"I just realized I didn't know what you were going to school for. We never really talked about it. You just mentioned some classes one night at dinner with your mother."

"Oh, um, yeah, I plan to get my masters in child psychology after I finish undergrad, and then hopefully eventually my doctorate."

"That's very admirable," he says, his tone sincere and genuine, like he's proud of me. Why does that make my chest squeeze?

I shrug. "I just find it an interesting field of study and enjoy working with children. I'd like to be a developmental therapist. I think there's a lot of kids, and parents out there who struggle because they don't know what is causing their child to be upset or what challenges they're facing and how to help. I'd like to be able to make things easier for them."

"Did you have any challenges as a child?" The words come out slowly as if he's not sure he should be asking.

"I got diagnosed with ADHD as a kid. Struggled in school. It wasn't severe, but it made things for my mom and me more challenging, and the doctor we had really helped. I also have something called auditory processing disorder, which is kind of what it sounds like. I have trouble processing spoken information sometimes, like it actually goes in one ear and out the other. It's just harder to understand because my brian and my ears don't coordinate. One way I've heard it described is like a tape playing too fast, so the words are going at a faster speed than my ears can process them."

"Did you get treatment?" he asks. I nod.

"I had a specialized education plan in school. They had special headphones for me that helped reduce background noise to make it easier for me to hear what the teacher was saying. I had some auditory therapy, and I brought recording devices with me to school."

"Do you have a specialized plan in college?"

"Not officially, but I've talked with some of my professors in the classes I'm struggling with more and they've been really good about helping me out. Giving me extra time for tests or letting me be in a quiet room by myself."

He nods. "That you want to go through so much extra schooling even with your diagnosis is impressive. That doesn't frighten you?"

"Maybe a little. I think it will be more of a challenge for me, but I can't let it keep me from doing what I want to do. And I'll be that much prouder of myself when I've accomplished what I've set out to."

"Indeed," he replies.

He goes back to his book and a while later we're pulling up to my surprise visit. He's so engrossed in his book he's not even aware we stopped until I unbuckle and stand, then take the kindle out of his hands and set it aside as he looks up at me, frowning.

"What are you doing? I was reading that!" He reaches for it and I pull it away again, laughing and gesturing out the window. He turns and his eyes widen at the beautiful lush flower garden we're parked outside of. I found out about it while searching for places to stop between Philly and Baltimore and knew Oliver would love it. It's got multiple different gardens, each with gorgeous plants, trees, and flowers arranged in what they call districts. The pictures online were stunning, but as we walk into the Hillside Garden, one of the many on the premises, I'm stunned by the gorgeous scenery and the pathway dusted with moss, winding through the six acre garden. There's the sound of waterfalls in the distance as we walk, hand in hand, through the tranquil landscape.

After Hillside Garden we visit Oak and Conifer Knoll, which houses majestic, ancient trees in a sprawling park-like landscape.

When we reach the Conservatory District, which contains an array of plants in rooms of 19th century classical architecture, Oliver's eyes widen in wonder. It's like watching a child on Christmas morning. He's enraptured, and I love watching him move around the space in awe. He marvels at the architectural landscaping in Cascade Garden, and I wonder what it would be like for him to do something like this. Something that makes him truly come alive. He hasn't said a word since we've entered, but I don't mind at all because I know he's taking it all in and I want him to enjoy every moment.

The indoor children's garden is adorable and charming and looks like something you would see in a fairytale, with its fountain and balconies. There's an Orchid House, a Waterlily Court, and more.

When we leave more than three hours later, my feet are sore and my legs ache, but I've never seen Oliver look so happy. I grunt when he spins me to him the moment we step onto the sidewalk again, and kisses me.

"Thank you," he murmurs against my lips. "That was wonderful."

I rest my hand on his cheek and kiss him again, even as people walk past us. "You're welcome," I say.

We return to the RV and head back out on the road. It's

only a couple more hours to Baltimore and a Cracker Barrel for Oliver. We're both hungry enough that we have lunch on the road and decide we'll save Cracker Barrel for dinner.

"Would you like me to drive?" Oliver asks, no doubt sensing how tired I am.

"You don't mind?" I say, and he shakes his head, so I gratefully take the passenger seat and doze off for a bit while he takes the wheel.

I wake to my phone ringing, and when I see that it's Mom Facetiming me, I answer it. I've been sending her pictures and we've texted a few times back and forth but haven't talked on the phone yet.

"You guys having fun?" she asks, and I rotate the screen so she can see Oliver driving. He gives a quick wave and a smile. Not the warm, bright, genuine one he gives me, I notice. The one that meets his eyes and makes him look so fucking sexy. No, this is his fake smile. The one he's been wearing for years, the one that he breaks out when he's trying to be happy, and I feel a pang in my chest.

"Yeah, it's been really great," I tell her. I know I should feel more guilt than I do. What I'm doing to her, what I'm risking, it's cruel and she doesn't deserve it. She's been an amazing mom. But I can't ignore what I feel for Oli, even if it's only temporary. Even if it ruins everything. I will never feel wrong for having him, for wanting him.

We don't talk for long, but I update her on our adventures, and when I hang up the phone, I sigh and run a hand through my hair.

"She sounds stressed and tired," Oliver says after a moment. I murmur my assent.

"Do you feel guilty?" I ask him.

"Yes," is his quick reply. I'm not surprised. If he didn't feel guilty for what we're doing he wouldn't be Oliver. Wouldn't be the man I'm coming to adore. His eyes are sad when he adds, "but I need you more than I feel guilty. You're the only bright thing in my life. The only thing I've ever done for myself. And if I had to do it all over again I wouldn't change anything that's happened between us. But please don't do this if you won't be able to live with yourself afterwards, Hunter. I'm not worth that. And I don't want to be the cause of your pain."

"I think it's too late for that, Oli," I tell him softly.

Eleven

HUNTER

It's evening when we arrive at Cracker Barrel for dinner. Oliver plays the peg board game at the table half a dozen times at least and pouts each and every time he has more than two pegs left at the end, but doesn't stop playing.

When we finish and make our way to the campground, it's almost dusk. The campsite is beautiful, and spacious, and along with a lake and hiking trails like the last campsite, it also has a pool and its own ice cream shop.

After getting everything hooked up we go for a dip in the lake, then head inside to shower.

He's sipping tea as he reads, standing near the stove, and I can't help smiling when I see him. He looks content, and I wish it could always be this way between us, because even though I know better, I am falling hard for this beautiful man. I just wish he could see himself the way I see him. I can't imagine growing up in a home that ingrained into you your entire life that who you are is wrong, the self loathing that would fester, the internal anguish and shame he must have been living with as a result. That's the trouble with people who are against homosexuality, they see it as a choice, as if picking a partner were the same as picking a school or a car or a home. But it's not a choice. No one would choose to be persecuted for being their authentic self. No one would choose to be the victim of hate crimes, to be shunned, excommunicated, or kicked out of their homes. No one would choose to have their basic human rights taken from them, because of who they love. And that Oliver has been hiding himself for so long makes me want to wring his parents' necks for ever making him believe he is anything less than worthy. The lengths he must have had to go to, both mentally and physically, to protect himself, make my chest ache. He deserves to be his true self, to chase his own happiness, without worrying about what anyone else thinks. I wish I could give him so much more than what I have on this trip.

I move up behind him and slip my arms around his waist, pressing my lips to his neck. He hums and leans against me, setting his kindle and his tea down on the counter. The thought of letting him go in a few more weeks breaks my heart. He's made me feel things I've never felt before, for anyone. I have such a strong desire to protect him, care for him, and nurture him, to watch him grow into the best possible version of himself, because I've seen glimpses of it on this trip, and it's beautiful.

"Hey," I whisper, pressing kisses to the freckles on his ear and feeling him shiver against me. My cock is already hard and pressed up against his ass. "You up for trying something a little bit different tonight?"

He nods. "Always. What did you have in mind?"

"I'd like you to top me," I tell him. His breath hitches and he turns to face me.

"You want me to fuck you?" he asks with an air of astonishment.

I nod. "Yes, Oli, I want you to fuck me." I kiss him, then reach between us and grip his semi hard cock, stroking it through his sweats. I'm hard as steel now, my cock pressed against his thigh. "I want this big beautiful cock inside me. I don't want to go another second without knowing what being filled by you is like."

He swallows and nods, a moan escaping him as I stroke him until he's fully erect. "I'm gonna ride you, baby," I tell him. "You okay with that?"

He nods again and I take his hand, leading him towards the bed. We strip and he lies on his back. I reach into my luggage and pull out a pair of leather handcuffs, showing them to him. I lick my lips when his cock twitches at the sight.

"Is this okay?" I ask, moving up his body and straddling him, his huge cock leaking onto his stomach already with how turned on he is.

"Yes," he says, breathless.

I slip his wrists inside and fasten them. "Use your safe word if you need to, if you decide you don't like them or if anything else makes you uncomfortable."

He nods again.

"I want to ride you while you lie there and watch me. Hands stay above your head, okay? No touching yourself or me. Understand?"

Another nod and twitch of his cock. "Good boy," I tell him, and his breath hitches, his hips arching upwards as precum oozes from his tip.

I grab the lube and reach back. I start to stretch myself as he gazes at me, his cock twitching again and again, his hips bucking and his breathing growing heavier. "Fuck, I...I want to see you," he grunts out. "Please?"

I press a kiss to his lips, then rotate myself so my ass is facing him, before I slip two fingers inside now, and he groans. "Oh, fuck, that's hot," he says. "Christ, Hunter, you're beautiful."

I slide a third finger inside and moan at the feeling of fullness. I haven't bottomed in a long time, but I want it with Oliver, more than anything.

"Shit, please," he whimpers. "I need you."

I slide my fingers out and turn to him, pressing another kiss to his full lips and stroking my fingers through his hair. His face is flushed, and I press kisses to the freckles on his nose, making him squirm. "Fuck yourself on me," he begs, and it's so earnest and sexy, his voice a low rumble, that my cock jerks and my hole spasms. I grab the condom and slide it on his shaft.

Then I'm lining myself up with his cock, and he gasps as his tip presses against my hole, then slowly pushes inside as I lower myself, feeling an intense burn as he slips past my ring, stretching me, filling me. I breathe out, then in, then out again before lowering myself a little bit more. "God, you're huge," I gasp, feeling like he's splitting me in two. I've never been this full before. It's incredible. I slide up again, and back down, letting him sink in a little further.

"Christ, that's hot," he murmurs, then groans, his head tilting back and his eyes closing as he bottoms out. "Shit, that's good."

"Oh, God," I moan, my own head tilted back now, as I rest my hands on his stomach, the pain giving way to unspeakable pleasure. "Fuck, Oli, you feel amazing. So full. So damn full. Your cock is so fucking incredible."

His cock jerks inside me and I moan. "So perfect, baby, " I croon. "You're gonna make me come so hard."

He whimpers, and I lean over to kiss him, before pushing myself up and lowering back down on his shaft, my nerve endings lighting up as his cock spears me again and again. "Oh, God, Oli," I whine, my fingers gripping his hair. "So good, so fucking good, baby."

I adjust my angle ever so slightly and then rise up and back down and his cock hits my prostate perfectly each time, my body shaking with pleasure. "Yes," I cry as I ride him, my eyes closed. "God, yes, Oli."

He whimpers as I fuck myself on him, each press of his cock against my prostate bringing me ecstasy like I've never known. "I'm gonna come, beautiful," I tell him as I rise and fall, my cock hard and aching, bouncing against my belly. "Fuck, Oli, I'm gonna come so hard. You feel so good. Love your big beautiful cock, baby."

I throw my head back and howl as my orgasm crashes into me and I spurt my release all over Oliver's stomach and chest. "Bloody hell," he gasps, his body shaking.

"Come for me," I rasp. "Fuck, Oli, let me feel you fill me up." He thrusts his hips twice and then I feel his cock pulsing inside me, the warmth of his release filing the condom as he throws his head back, his neck muscles straining and his eyes closed, sweat beading his brow.

I reach up and remove the handcuffs from his wrists before collapsing on top of him. His fingers are running through my hair seconds later, before he presses a kiss to the top of my head.

"Fuck, that was sexy as hell," he murmurs, and I nod in agreement, relaxing completely as I rest on his warm body, breathing him in, the hairs on his chest and abdomen tinged with sweat, soft and warm against my bare skin.

It's so comfortable I don't want to get up, but I make myself after a few minutes and clean us both off, before climbing back into bed. Oliver takes me in his arms and we fall asleep naked and sated.

OLIVER

The following day we visit the National Aquarium, and the day after that we peruse the Baltimore Museum of Art. We take a tour of the Edgar Allan Poe House and Museum another day. After visiting the George Peabody Library, we have dinner at a local seafood restaurant, and then take a stroll along National Harbor, breathing in the salty sea air and listening to the birds squawk and the waves crashing on the shore. We catch an outdoor showing of Charlie and the Chocolate Factory on the Potomac and take an evening ride on the Capital Wheel.

That evening after dinner, we lay on the blanket outside our trailer together and stare up at the stars. There's so many of them, and I find them utterly enchanting. I haven't star gazed, really since I was a child and Olivia and I would sneak out onto the roof outside of her bedroom window when our parents thought we were asleep, and sit there, just staring up at the endless night sky, and making wishes. Some out loud and others to ourselves.

"You ever wished upon a star?" I ask Hunter, and he turns to me.

"Have you?" he says, and I nod.

"What did you wish for?"

"Oh, many things. Things every child wishes for probably. A teddy bear, a dog, a new bike."

"Did any come true?"

I give a soft smile. "The teddy bear, and the new bike did happen eventually."

"No dog, though?"

"No. My parents were never fond of animals. Said they were too much work, too dirty, too expensive." I sigh, "which they are, I'm sure, but I was convinced the negatives were far fewer than the positives. I loved the idea of having someone be excited to see me when I came home from school. Someone to run and play with, other than my sister, someone to pet and cuddle when I was sick or sad. I think I just really wanted to feel loved and less alone."

He reaches over and slides his fingers through mine, squeezing my hand. He doesn't say anything, but he doesn't need to. He's listening to things I've never told anyone before. And it feels good, therapeutic even to talk to him, to share.

"What would you name a dog if you had one?" he asks.

"Clifford," I say, and he laughs.

"Like the big red dog?"

"Of course, he's fantastic, and I loved those books as a child. Our nanny would read them to us and they became favorites of mine."

"They are fun," he agrees.

"You never answered the question," I point out.

He hums, pondering. "I don't think I ever wished on a star. I was too practical for that."

"You mean dull?" I quip, and he laughs.

"Do you like dogs, or animals in general?"

"Yeah, I do. We never had one either, though. Mom was always too busy."

"Will you get one when you're finished with school?"

"Maybe."

We lie in comfortable silence again before he says, "You have a favorite color?"

I smile. "Green."

"Like lime green, or forest green, or like bad diarrhea green?"

"Diarrhea green?" I say, picking my head up off the blanket. "Is that how people describe it?"

He laughs and shrugs. "I don't know, maybe olive green is a better description."

I laugh, too. "Maybe? God, I don't think you've set the bar very high with diarrhea. You would be hard pressed to find something worse." He laughs again and it's so warm and vibrant that it makes my entire body tingle.

"I would say dark green and emerald green, probably. You?"

"Orange."

"Like orange, orange, or pumpkin orange, or red orange?" He smirks at me and I chuckle.

"Like, sunrise orange," he says, thoughtfully. "Like new beginnings and possibilities."

I hum, stroking my thumb over his hand still clinging to mine. "Tell me more," I say, and he looks at me again.

"Like what?"

"I don't know. All of it. What's your favorite candy? Do you like mustard or ketchup on your hot dogs? Baked or mashed potatoes? Fruit salad or regular salad? What's your favorite season? Do you prefer snow or rain? What makes you happy, what infuriates you, what thrills you and what drives you bonkers. I want to know it all."

He stares at me, and I wonder if I've gone too far, but then he smiles and says, "Nerds."

I blink. "Pardon?"

"My favorite candy. It's nerds. I hate mustard on anything, love ketchup. But mixing mayo and ketchup together and dunking fries in them is the best. Mashed potatoes all the way, and I like both types of salad."

I grin, for whatever reason utterly delighted at the knowledge that I get to know these simple things about him, things that perhaps are insignificant in the grand scheme of things, but to me are so utterly priceless, because it's him. It's what makes Hunter who he is, and who he is, is someone I am very much realizing that I never want to stop getting to know. I find myself terrified of that prospect but so incapable of drawing away, like I should be. The emotional attachment I feel to him is like nothing I've ever known, the desire to hold fast to him and not let go. I know I should stop this, right here right now, just stick to the sex and stop sharing these intimate moments, because the more we talk about life and dreams and favorites, the more I don't want this trip to end. The more I want him. But I've not been able to do the things I should do since the moment I met him. So with every answer he gives me, I find myself cherishing it, soaking it up, savoring it, and waiting on bated breath for more, always more of him. "Favorite season?"

"Summer. Maybe just because I get a break from school, though," he says with a chuckle. "And I know it's hot, but I've never minded the heat, and I love swimming. I don't know, everything just feels slower, somehow, and I like that. The peacefulness of it all. And I love rain, which there's a lot of in the summer, so. You?"

"Oh, I much prefer snow to rain. Though I don't enjoy driving in either. But snow is friendlier in my opinion."

"Friendlier?" he says with a laugh.

"Well, it doesn't drench you or pelt you in the face, does it?" I reply. "It's much gentler, softer. You won't get very wet when it snows unless you want to go playing in it. Rain is just ruthless. It's all about consent." He laughs at that and I grin. "As far as seasons go, I don't know, I think I've honestly just been so focused on work I don't notice the difference much, especially now, working from home. I do enjoy the flowers in spring, though."

"And what makes you happy?" he asks, referencing my earlier question to him, then drawing my hand to his lips and pressing soft kisses to each finger, making my breath hitch.

"Being here, with you," I tell him. "I've never been happier."

We spend the next couple of days enjoying the fresh air and sunshine around our campground; swimming, hiking, kayaking, and just relaxing. We have sex every evening, and while I have decided I prefer bottoming, I don't mind letting Hunter ride me either. He's a vision to behold when he's bouncing on my cock, chasing his pleasure, that toned, slender body on display.

On our last night in Baltimore, I sink to my knees in front of Hunter as he sits on the sofa, reading, and slide his Kindle out of his hands like he's done to me several times on this trip.

When he looks up, his eyes widen slightly at the sight of me. "Hello," he says, and I flush.

"I uh…I was hoping you might let me blow you."

He grins and leans forward, gripping my chin and pressing a kiss to my lips. "You may," he says.

"Just to clarify, I've never actually given anyone a blow job before, so this will probably be terrible. I feel like you should be privy to that knowledge before we begin."

His eyes twinkle with amusement and he lifts his hips, shucking off his sweats and leaving only his bikini briefs, showcasing his half hard cock. My mouth waters and my own cock thickens in my shorts as I stare at him.

"I'm ready when you are," he says. "Don't worry about it being perfect, Oli. Just avoid using your teeth and try to relax."

I nod as I scoot forward between his splayed thighs and reach up to grip the waistband of his briefs. I pull them down just enough to let his cock and balls free, licking my lips at the sight of his hard cock leaking precum. I tuck the briefs under his balls and he moans, his cock jerking as he slides his fingers into my hair, gripping tightly before I've even gotten my mouth around him. My eyes dart up to meet his. "Relax," he tells me again. "Even if it's terrible I will enjoy it because it was you."

I nod, feeling my tension ease, then I grip his hip with one hand and begin to fondle his balls with the other as I lean forward and lick the salty precum from his tip, moaning around the taste as it explodes on my tongue. He hisses and jerks slightly, his dick twitching. "Christ, Oli, you look so good on your knees for me," he purrs.

I hum and lick his tip again, before pressing kisses to his head and watching as more precum leaks out and slides down his shaft, his stomach rising and falling, his cock hardening with each press of my lips to his heated skin, until he's gripping my hair so hard it makes me squeak. He doesn't say anything. I think he wants me to go at my own pace, even if it's driving him crazy. He wants me to explore, discover, and enjoy the experience, not be rushed.

My hands play with his balls still, rolling them and then tugging as I slide my mouth over just the tip of his erection and suck gently before swirling my tongue over his slit. Then I'm taking him deeper, but I don't make it more than halfway down his length before I feel my gag reflex kicking in, so I stay there, moving up and down on his cock, never taking him all the way in, my head bobbing as I shift my hand from his balls to his dick to stroke the base. I moan when his cock jerks inside me.

"Fuck," he grunts, his hips thrusting slightly, making his cock slide a bit deeper. My eyes start to water but I don't stop. I can't. I want this. I need it. I need him, his taste filling me, the weight of him on my tongue, in my hand. His release sliding down my throat when he reaches the peak of his pleasure, his cock spasming inside me. The thought makes me moan around him and his cock jerks again.

His voice is raspy when he says, "Fuck, Oli. Love your mouth, baby. You feel amazing around my cock."

His praise has me soaring and sliding my mouth even further down his shaft, my other hand returning to his balls, tugging and rolling them as before. I look up at him as he stares down at me, his beautiful face blurred by my tears. He starts to thrust into my mouth gently and I hum around him, making him grip my hair in both hands as his head falls back. His thrusts pick up speed and I have tears streaming down my cheeks, nostrils flaring and nose running as he fucks my face.

"Gonna come," he cries. "God, Oli, yes, so good, baby. Gonna fill that pretty mouth." He thrusts three more times before his cock pulses and he's spilling his release down my throat. I gag a little but swallow as much as I can, savoring the taste of him and the knowledge that I got him off with my mouth.

"Fuck," he breathes when he slides out of me. "You took me so well, baby." He grabs a tissue and wipes the snot and tears from my face before pressing a kiss to my lips.

"Did I do okay?" I ask.

"So good," he praises, and I believe him.

Twelve

OLIVER

I moan the next morning when I feel a cold wet finger pressing inside my hole and then Hunter's soft, warm lips against my thighs as my eyes flutter open. I spread my legs for him and he kisses me.

"Morning, beautiful," he murmurs against my lips. I groan as he adds a second finger and scissors them, prepping me for his cock. His other hand slides up my thigh and his lips press to my knees. "Wanna try something new today. You game?"

I moan as he slips a third finger inside me. "Yes," I gasp.

He grins. "I'm gonna take a bit longer stretching you because you're going to get double stuffed today, baby."

My eyes widen. "What?"

"I have a toy I want to use on you, a dildo, and I want to be inside you at the same time." He presses more kisses to my legs as he continues to stretch me. "You can safeword at any time if it gets to be too much, but I think you'll like it."

I nod and moan again as his fingers move inside me. It already feels so damn good. He nudges my prostate a couple of times and my cock oozes precum. He spends a couple more minutes stretching me with his fingers before he slides out of me all the way and I whimper at the loss.

He grabs the toy, a large bright pink silicone dildo with ridges and different sized bumps running the length of it. It's as long as me but not quite as thick. He slicks it up with lube and I spread my legs wider, feeling my hole flutter in anticipation. "Ready, baby?" he asks, pressing it gently against my entrance.

I nod, my hands gripping my legs to keep them spread wide for him. "Yes, please."

"Love when you beg," he purrs, then kisses me, before pushing on the dildo and letting it slip inside me, making me moan as it brushes against my nerve endings. My thighs shake as he shoves it in, inch by inch. "God, that's hot. Jesus, Oli."

I preen at his praise and moan again as he slides it out a little and back in, lighting up those nerve endings once more and making my cock throb. He does it again before he's planting kisses to my thighs and purring, "So pretty, Oli. You look so good stuffed full with a toy." He moves it out a little before pushing it back inside, and it hits my prostate, making me buck and shout.

He repeats the gesture several times until I'm whimpering. "Christ, Hunter, I need you. Please. Need your cock."

He leaves the toy inside me and slides on a condom before slicking himself up with lube. Then he's at my entrance and I can't believe I'm going to have his cock inside me along with the dildo.

"What if I can't?" I say, my skin prickling with nerves. "You're not small either, and the toy…"

"You can," he assures me, running his fingers through my hair. "You can do it, Oli. You can take it."

I nod. I believe him, and even more importantly I trust him to take care of me. He pushes against my hole and I gasp as my body accepts the intrusion. Fuck, I've never felt anything like this before. I feel like a Thanksgiving turkey, stuffed to the brim. It burns for several moments as my body adjusts to having both cocks inside me. Hunter rubs his hands along my stomach and legs in a soothing gesture. "So good," he says. "So good for me, my sweet Oliver."

The combination of his words and the incredible pressure inside me has tears stinging at the corners of my eyes. "Fuck," I cry, then gasp in pleasure as my body loosens and he slides all the way inside. I can't stop moaning at the incredible plea- sure that overwhelms me, at how full I feel, how owned, how utterly and completely taken.

Hunter breathes out as he slides both himself and the dildo out slightly and then back in. I have my hands up on either side of my head, my eyes closed and mouth parted in bliss as he fucks me with the dildo and his cock. I already know I'll be coming hands free. It feels so good with each and every thrust I don't need to touch myself.

"God, you feel amazing," he rumbles. "You look so damn hot like this, Oli. Stuffed to the brink. Your hole is so perfect, baby."

I gasp and buck my hips when his angle changes slightly and he pegs my prostate again and again. "Oh, God. I need to come," I cry.

"Do it, baby," Hunter tells me. He thrusts himself and the dildo inside me two more times and I'm spraying hard, my back arching, my head thrown back, my cock pulsing load after load of my release all over my stomach and chest, some even landing on my chin. I don't think I've ever come so hard in my life. God, that was amazing.

"Fuck, yeah, baby," Hunter grunts, "so damn hot." Then he's slipping out of me and pulling off the condom, but leaving the dildo inside as he kneels between my legs and strokes himself hard and fast, before his load joins mine, covering my naked body. He leans over and laps up the sticky mess, moaning around it, before gripping my hair and pressing his mouth to mine.

HUNTER

After dozing for a brief moment we get up and shower before eating breakfast and then making the drive to Bethany Beach in Delaware. After this it will be Atlantic City and then back home. And I can't help wishing we could extend the trip so I could spend more time with him, let him be himself for just a while longer. I hate the idea of returning home and watching him shrink back into himself, when the real him is so vibrant and beautiful.

We catch a movie on the beach at dusk that evening after we arrive. The following morning we visit the local farmers market where we pick up some fresh vegetables and local honey for Oliver's tea. Seeing the fresh flowers reminds me of the bouquet I got for him and how much he loves it. I have caught him smelling it a few times when he thinks I'm not looking. Such a small gesture, to make him so happy.

We enjoy swimming more, and I don't think I'll ever get enough of him in that red speedo. He hasn't gone back to his regular trunks since the first day, and I can see how much more confident he is in his body. Every part of him is a masterpiece, just waiting to be discovered.

On our third night there I take him to bed again, desperate for him, for his body; desperate to touch and kiss, and caress; desperate to feel him around me, to be inside him, knowing our time is coming to an end, and so overwhelmed with emotion I can barely breathe. I knew this was short term. I knew we were on borrowed time, but my heart didn't get the memo apparently, because it wants so much more. I want so much more.

I pepper him with kisses as I make love to him, his legs wrapped around me and our bodies slick with sweat.

Holding him in my arms afterwards is as delicious as it is painful. Because I don't know how to let him go.

We spend one final day relaxing around the campsite, walking the trails, even catching some fish to grill for supper. Oliver cooks it with a splash of olive oil, some lemon juice, a sprinkle of parsley, minced garlic and salt and pepper. It's wonderful.

That night I coax him to bed again and his eyes light up when I bring out the handcuffs and another toy.

"I'd like to try something a little different," I tell him, showing him the prostate massager. Since he loved the last toy we used, I'm hoping he'll find this one just as stimulating. "I want to put this inside you, and then I will be controlling it from my phone. I want to say some things, and have you repeat them. If you do, it will vibrate inside you. You may come at any time, but you won't get the pleasure of the massager unless you repeat what I say, and you are not allowed to touch yourself."

He nods.

"Color?" I ask.

"Green," he replies. I smile and stretch him for a moment before slicking the toy up and pushing it inside him. He swallows it greedily and moans as it fills him, his cock hard and heavy between his legs. I press a button that allows the head of the massager to rotate inside him and he mewls, his cock spasming as precum leaks down his shaft and his hips buck.

"Fuck!" he shouts.

"Good?" I say, and he nods.

"More." His voice is so needy it has my cock growing hard.

"Repeat what I say and you can have more," I remind him. "Ready?"

He nods again, but then his brows furrow when I say, "My name is Oliver Jones."

"What?" he starts, but I hold up a hand. He swallows.

"My name is Oliver Jones," he repeats, and I press the

button on my phone, his cries of pleasure echoing throughout the small space as the toy goes off inside him. "Fuck," he pants.

"I am thirty-six years old," I say, and he looks at me as his chest rises and falls. I won't make him say anything he doesn't want to say. He can safeword at any time.

"I am thirty-six years old," he says, his voice softer than the last time, and I press the button again. It goes off until I press it, telling it to stop, and he's trembling, sweat clinging to his ivory skin. "Oh fuck, oh fuck, oh fuck," he gasps.

"I am a queer man," I say softly. He pauses longer this time, and I see the tears spring to his eyes. My Oliver. My sweet, beautiful, Oliver.

"I am…a queer man," he stutters out, in between sobs and I press the button again. His cock spasms as I let it go on for several moments before pressing it again to stop. His skin is flushed, his cheeks wet with tears.

"I am good," I say, and he closes his eyes and sobs, but eventually he repeats, "I am good." The toy goes off again and he bites his lip hard, his body shaking.

"I am worthy," I say, and he shakes his head. "I. Am. Worthy," I repeat gently. He squeezes his eyes shut as more tears fall, but says the words, his voice unsteady.

"I am enough, exactly as I am," I say, and tears are spilling down my cheeks now, too. There's a long pause before I say, "You don't have to believe it, Oliver, you just have to say it. Believing it will come with time."

There's an even longer pause before he chokes out, "I am enough, exactly as I am." He curses and screams my name when I press the button this time. He cries more.

"I am allowed to disappoint my parents," I whisper, and wonder if he heard me when he doesn't respond. But then he says it, too, and I press the button again.

"Please," he sobs. "Please, Hunter." I don't even know what he's asking for and I don't think he does either, because he can come whenever he wants, he knows that. His cock is straining, and I can tell he's close, ready to explode as soon as I hit the button again.

But when I say, with my chest heaving, "I promise to chase my own happiness, even if it means I lose people in the process," his eyes squeeze shut again, before his gaze locks with mine, and with a choked sob he says one word.

"Red."

Thirteen

HUNTER

I go to him as soon as the word leaves his mouth. As quickly as I can, I undo the cuffs and let him free, then slide the prostate massager out, setting it aside. I gather him in my arms and hold him as he curls into a ball, sobs wracking his body.

"I'm here, Oli," I tell him. "You're safe, baby. I'm right here."

I hold him for hours and he cries himself to sleep.

Fourteen

HUNTER

Oliver is quiet the next morning. I'm up first, like usual, and make his tea for him. He drinks it, giving me a small appreciative smile when I hand it to him, but he doesn't say anything. We eat mostly in silence, him only breaking it to ask how long it will take to reach Atlantic City.

"Three hours," I tell him, and he nods.

"Want me to drive?" he asks, but he can't be serious. There's no way after the events of last night I'm going to let him get behind the wheel.

"No, I can do it." He nods again and then moves to take a shower, leaving his dishes in the sink. I wash them and put them away while he dresses, hating how the atmosphere has changed between us.

I don't know if last night actually helped him in any way like I'd hoped it would, or if I've simply caused more emotional damage to a man who has dealt with enough trauma to last him a lifetime.

"Oli?" I say when we're finally on the road and he's staring out the window. "If you need to take a nap or anything, you can. I'll be fine. You don't need to keep me company." I see him wiping his cheek through the window and feel a pang in my chest.

When he turns he gives me a sad smile. "I'm okay."

I don't press him further. I have a feeling whatever last night was for him he's still processing it and isn't ready to talk. He may never be ready to talk, at least not to me.

It's the longest three hours of my life, but finally we make it to Atlantic City. Part of me is tempted to just drive straight home and forget staying here, but I can't bring myself to do it. Not only am I exhausted but I'm fucking selfish, and not ready to let my time with Oliver be over. Sure, if we wanted to we could still fuck back home when Mom is at work, and even though we probably will, it's not the same.

Oliver makes us dinner again, and we eat outside. He reads and sips his tea afterwards, still barely speaking but he seems to have perked up a little bit. I just wish I knew how to help him. It kills me that he's hurting so much.

Mom Facetimes again to tell us she is looking forward to seeing us in a couple of days.

"You, too, love," Oliver tells her, that fake smile ever present.

He runs his hand through his hair after we hang up and then tells me he's tired and heading to bed early. When I get to the bed a couple of hours later I can tell he's still awake, but don't say anything. I hesitate, not knowing if I should scoot closer and hold him, but I can't not.

I shuffle over and curl into him, draping my arm over his body and letting his ass rest against my crotch, his back pressed to my chest. I hear his breath hitch slightly but don't say anything. Only seconds later, he's snoring softly.

I let Oliver sleep in the next morning. We're not in any rush. When he wakes he seems to be doing better. And though it's small I even get one of his genuine smiles.

I have blueberry muffins ready for him along with his tea, as well as strawberries and melon, which he eats a healthy serving of.

We shower and then make our way out into the city. I hadn't planned it, but since Oliver has been feeling so down lately I decided to take us to a spa. I think he could use some pampering and he deserves it. We get massages and then facials afterwards, and when we leave he seems almost back to his normal self.

We eat lunch out and do some shopping on the board-walk, then head to a drag show taking place that evening. Oliver seems a little hesitant at the idea but he's relaxing and smiling as soon as we walk inside.

We sleep curled up again that night and the next day we relax at our campsite, swimming, fishing, and soaking up the sun.

After dinner, I'm sitting with his head in my lap as we watch the sun disappear behind the trees. It's been a wonderful day and my heart is so full my chest feels like it will burst with how much he means to me. I know he might not be ready to hear it, he may never be ready to hear it, but I can't let this trip end without him knowing how I feel. Maybe it's foolish, because it won't matter in the end anyway. He's still engaged to Mom and even though we've been enjoying ourselves on this trip I have no reason to believe his feelings for me go as deeply as mine for him. But maybe if he knows he won't make the biggest mistake of his life. So even if it's selfish, I stroke my fingers through his hair, my heart pound-ing, and say, "Oli?"

He looks up at me, "Hmm?"

The words catch on my tongue and I clear my throat. Why is fucking him and calling him my good boy so much easier than this?

Because I'm not risking my heart, that's why.

But as I sit there and look into pale blue eyes and a freckle scattered face I realize it doesn't matter, my heart stopped being mine the day I met him. I've been fucked this whole time, because Oliver fucking Jones doesn't just own my heart, he is my goddamn heart. "Oli, I...I think I'm—"

He jerks upright and rolls away so fast I barely have time to blink or realize what's happening before he's standing and brushing his pants off, stuttering, "I'm tired. I'm sorry, I...I'm going to head to bed. Goodnight, Hunter."

I don't even have the chance to respond before he's inside and I'm left sitting there alone, feeling more foolish and hurt than I have in a long time. Tears slide down my cheeks and I wipe them away.

"I love you," I whisper into the night. And of course, there's no answer.

If I thought the three hour trip to Atlantic City was miserable it's nothing compared to the two hour one back to Scarsdale. I don't think this trip could have ended on a more miserable note. Oliver won't even look at me, and it's so painful I want to fucking scream. Scream at him to live his own life, to let me love him, to be the man I know he is. The one who's brave, and kind, and caring, and who is an absolute pillow princess. The one who loves gay romance and stargazing and holding my hand. The one who thrives on praise and loves being the small spoon. The one who loves plants and has a childlike curiosity about him that melts my heart. I don't want him to lose himself when he's finally just found himself.

It's lunch time when we arrive back home. We return the RV and settle into the house, each going to our separate rooms to unpack. I turn with a start when I hear a knock on my door frame. He's standing there like he hasn't been ignoring me all day. Like I didn't try to tell him I love him and have him run away like his pants were on fire.

"I can make us lunch, if you—" he starts

"Don't marry her," I say, and his eyes widen, his shoulders tensing. "Don't marry her, Oli," I repeat and tears fill my eyes.

He's across the room in seconds, gripping my face and kissing me so hard I forget to breathe. But God, it's everything. It's all of his passion and fervor and strength poured into one earth shattering kiss. I cry harder as I pull away from him because this isn't a hello kiss. It's a goodbye kiss. I press my fingers to his lips as I sob.

"One more time," he begs. "Please, baby, just one more time. I won't ask for more than that. I know this isn't fair to you. I need you, Hunter. I need to be your good boy one more time."

"Fuck you," I whisper as tears slide down my cheeks. He pulls me to him and our lips crash together again, heated, frenzied, biting, whimpering as we pull at each other's clothes before we fall onto my bed, naked, and I slip inside him. One more time. One more time to kiss him, one more time to hold him, to love him, to breathe in the smell of him, to taste him, and worship him.

He clings to me like he never has before and I wrap my arms around him, holding him to me as I bury myself inside him, wishing I could stay forever. When we come, it's together, his legs wrapped around me and our bodies so entangled I don't know where he ends and I begin. I kiss him through my tears and then pull out, lying next to him. He reaches over and wipes my cheeks, but more tears fall.

"Don't marry her," I repeat. "I love you, Oli. I fucking love you."

"No, you—"

"Don't do that," I say, shaking my head, my jaw clenched and my voice stormy. "Don't you dare tell me that what I feel for you isn't love. Don't do that to me, you fucking bastard."

He starts, but gathers himself quickly. "Hunter…" He says it in a tone that isn't at all affectionate. He sounds like a fucking teacher scolding me for starting a fight in class.

"No!" I shout, then scramble out of bed. "I can't do this,

Oliver. Not for two more weeks, not for a single fucking day. Fuck you in the light of day but then watch you go to her room at night, knowing you're on the other side of that door with your cock buried inside her. God, Oli, I want to rip my fucking hair out just thinking about you fucking her." I'm sobbing as I shout at him. "It was hard enough when I was infatuated with you, but being in love with you and knowing what you two are doing in there every night? I can't."

"She's a good person, Hunter," he starts, pushing himself up to sit, and I see red.

"Who fucking cares?!" I shout. "She doesn't even fucking know you!" His eyes widen and his face pales, but I don't fucking care if I've upset him, or made him uncomfortable. He's done the same to me, and I'm fucking pissed and done with his bullshit. "Does she know you like to be fucked, Oliver? Does she know you like to be told how good you are, that you like to be held down and manhandled? That you would rather be fucked than fuck someone else? Does she know how you melt when you are praised? Because I do! That's mine! You are fucking mine, Oliver!" My chest heaves as my voice breaks. "And I'm yours. So don't fucking marry her."

He slides out of bed and slips his underwear back on before making his way to the door and opening it. "We should shower before your mom gets home," he says, his voice completely void of emotion, before he shuts the door behind him.

I bury my face in my pillow and scream.

Fuck, why didn't I think coming home would be this hard? Did I seriously believe that spending two weeks alone with Oliver would change everything? Or anything? That a man who has repressed his sexuality for twenty years would do a one-eighty and admit his feelings for me?

God, I am so fucking naive.

OLIVER

I'm shaking, and my heart is pounding so hard I can barely breathe while I let the warm water cascade over me. I barely made it out of there before the tears fell. He can't bloody love me. He can't. And he doesn't love the Oliver I've let everyone else see. The Oliver that Amanda loves. Even the Oliver my sister Olivia or my nephew Freddie loves, because I never let them see the real me. I never knew who the real me was until him.

Climbing out of the shower, I dry myself off, my body still trembling. I slip into sweats and a T-shirt, before I notice the folded white piece of paper lying next to the parrot I'd set on the bed. It has my name on it, and I know who it's from and what it probably says before I even pick it up.

Tears start sliding down my cheeks all over again as I pick it up, almost dropping it again because my hands are shaking so hard. I have to force myself to read when I open it.

Oliver,

I know you believe you are doing the right thing, and maybe you are. Maybe you and Mom can make each other happy. I honestly hope that you can, because you deserve it. You deserve everything you want. Knowing you has been the greatest joy of my life, and I will never regret the time we had. You are beautiful, and worthy, and good, and that's true no matter what parts of you you decide to share with the rest of the world. I will never forget you, Oli, but I have to go. I have to get over you, and I can't do that being here.

I hope you find your happiness, Oli, that you discover the limitless joy of being your true self, and letting the world accept you for exactly who you are, because you have hidden for long enough, and the world deserves the real you. You are my first and greatest love, Oliver Jones.

Love, Hunter

My tears are sliding down my cheeks and dripping onto the paper as I read, blurring the ink. I sit on the bed with the note in my hand, reading it again. "Bloody hell," I sob, and jump when I hear, "Bloody hell," from next to me.

"Oh, for Christ's sake, you demonic creature," I grouse, and reach over to turn him off yet again. How that bird keeps getting turned back on I don't know, and part of me wants to throw him up against the nearest wall, but I can't, even if he is fucking posessed, because Hunter gave him to me, and it and the flowers that are slowly dying are the only things I have left to remind me of our time together. And even though it's becoming a painful reminder, I'd rather have that than nothing.

I wipe my tears and try to pull myself together. I can't be a fucking mess when Amanda gets home. Folding the note up, I slide it inside my pants pocket. On my way down the hall I stop at Hunter's room, hoping that maybe he changed his mind after leaving the note and hasn't really gone anywhere. But his room is empty and his luggage that he'd carried upstairs is gone. He probably didn't even unpack, just closed everything back up and left.

When I make my way downstairs and the house is empty I feel an ache settling in my chest. I don't think I've ever felt so alone. Curling up on the sofa, I turn the television on and end up falling asleep.

I wake to fingers running through my hair, and for a moment I think it's Hunter. That he hasn't left, that it was all a nightmare and that he's here to care for me, to kiss me, to tell me I'm beautiful and good, because I miss his praise so much already. There's a kiss pressed to my forehead and I open my eyes, knowing before I do that it's not the Price that I want for it so desperately to be. No, it's the one I'm engaged to, smiling down at me as she continues to stroke her fingers through my hair.

"Hey, sleepy head," she says, sitting on the coffee table

across from me. "You must have been tired from all that driving. Sleep well?"

I nod. "Hunter?" I say, and I'm not sure why.

She smiles again. "He's gone, baby. He called and told me he had to get back to work early. You guys have a nice time?"

I nod. "I'm sorry you missed him."

"Yeah, me, too," she says. "He seemed a little off when he called, so I hope everything is okay."

I squeeze her hand and she stands. "I'm beat, and it seems like you are, too, so what about ordering in?"

I'm honestly not hungry at all, but it sounds better than cooking right now, so I nod again and she goes upstairs to change. I let her curl up next to me as we wait for dinner to arrive, and try to ask her about work and fill her in on the things Hunter and I did on our trip that she didn't know about yet. I excuse myself and return with the earrings I bought her and she fawns over them like I knew she would. But when she kisses me I can't help thinking that her lips against mine are all wrong. She tastes like the wine she drank with supper and the scent of her lemon and raspberry body wash fills my nostrils.

I have to make myself kiss her, telling myself that she is what I want. That I'll adjust, adapt, to someone else's flavor on my tongue, to someone else's arms around me, to someone else's lips on mine. I'll adjust to the idea of never being fucked again. Never having Hunter's hard cock inside me again, his hand pulling my hair in a way that made my cock throb each and every time, never feel his filthy words against my skin and endure his deliscious torture. But I'll adjust.

She asks about the parrot and the flowers when she sees them on the dresser and I tell her I purchased them on our trip. I don't know why I lie, but I can't bring myself to tell her that Hunter got them for me.

"I didn't know you liked sunflowers," she states as she smells them. "They're almost dead. Should we toss them?"

The thought makes me physically ill and I find myself

shaking my head. "Not yet." I don't give her any explanation beyond that.

She gives a soft smile and climbs into bed. "The parrot is cute."

I manage to smile back. "I thought Freddie might like to play with it when he comes over." She nods and kisses me.

But when she slides her hand down my pants I can't get hard. And I tell her I'm just still worn out and not feeling well, something I caught on the trip, probably.

She frowns slightly but presses a kiss to my head and curls up against me instead.

We go to my parents' house for supper the following evening, after I spend the day trying to work again and feeling so bloody depressed I don't think I accomplish a single thing. I'm struggling to focus and my mind is a foggy mess.

I know I'm poor company, though I try to engage while we eat, and Mother peppers us with questions about the wedding and asks Amanda about work.

"Oliver," I hear and jerk my head up, startled. My plate has barely been touched and all three sets of eyes are on me. For her part, Amanda's are filled with concern while my parents seem more irritated than anything else.

"Yes?" I ask.

"Amanda was telling us you went on a road trip with her son," Mother says. "Hunter, is it?"

I nod, but can't bring myself to share more.

"For Christ's sake, son, what's the matter with you?" Father says. "You're rather dull tonight."

Something about that comment makes me snap. "I'm sorry, Father, I didn't realize that it was my job to entertain you."

"Oliver," Amanda admonishes gently. "He's not feeling well," she tells them.

"Oh, why on earth not?" Father says.

"Would you like something?" Mother says. "We have Tylenol and Aspirin."

I shake my head, though I do have a headache brewing. "No, thank you." No amount of painkillers is going to solve my problem.

We leave shortly after dinner and Amanda drives us home. "Are you sure you're okay?" she asks on the way.

I reach over and take her hand, giving it a gentle squeeze. "I'm fine, love. I think I'm just worn out from the trip still, and work was difficult today. I just need some rest."

She doesn't come on to me that night, or suggest sex, but I know I can't avoid it forever. Tomorrow is Saturday so we'll sleep in and probably do some chores around the house that have been piling up, maybe buy groceries.

I feel like I'm existing in a fog, and I don't know how to snap out of it, but I miss Hunter so much it hurts to exist right now.

Amanda's in the kitchen when I make my way downstairs the next day. She sits at the table, sipping her coffee, and I go to her, pressing a kiss to her hair and squeezing her shoulder. She smiles up at me and rests her hand on mine.

"You slept in," she says, and I nod. When I woke and saw that it was nearly ten o'clock I couldn't believe it. Hunter was the early riser on our trips but I was always up by eight thirty. I must have needed it, though, and I do feel a bit more like myself today, though I'm honestly not sure what that means anymore, because who I am is still something I'm trying to figure out, or at least accept.

"I'm gonna start some laundry and then head to the store," she tells me as I set the kettle on the stove. "Then I thought we could get online and apply for our marriage license if you're up for that? We should do it sooner rather than later."

My throat constricts but I manage, "Of course, love."

She smiles at me, then finishes her coffee and heads back upstairs to collect the laundry, I assume. When she returns I'm sipping my tea.

"Oliver?" she says, her voice shaky, and my face goes ashen when I look up and see the paper she's holding in her hand. The letter that Hunter wrote me and that I foolishly shoved inside the pocket of my sweats. I'd completely forgotten about it when I put them in the washing basket. She looks as pale as I feel and her eyes are filled with tears as I set my cup aside, my hand trembling.

"What is this?" she asks, her chest heaving. "Hunter wrote this to you? My son wrote this to you?"

I don't know what to say. Everything in me wants to snatch the letter away from her because it's mine. It's private and the words on it are meant for me, not her. Not anyone else. But there's no getting out of this. I could lie, but I'm so sick of lying. My entire life has been a lie and it's utterly exhausting.

"Talk to me!" she shouts. Tears stream down her cheeks as she throws the note and lets it float in the air between us before it settles on the kitchen floor. "What is going on? Why the hell is my son leaving you a note, telling you he loves you after two fucking weeks? What the hell happened on that trip?"

I open my mouth but she points at me, her gaze fierce. "If you even think about lying to me, Oliver Jones, I swear to God..." her words trail off as she sobs again and I shake my head.

I grip her arm and she lets me pull her to the table where we both sit. She stares at me, confused, broken and angry, and I know I deserve all of her wrath and hatred, and so much more. Hunter was right. She doesn't deserve this, and I could have saved her so much pain and heartache if I'd been honest about everything sooner. If I'd told her the truth about me.

"Hunter and I met before the trip," I say. My chest

tightens because I can't believe I'm doing this, but she deserves the truth. She deserved it long before now. Tears start filling my eyes but I do my best to hold them back. I don't deserve to cry right now. I caused this. I'm the reason for all of this. She's sitting here now, devastated and humiliated because of me, and Hunter is gone right now because of me. I've fucked up so royally. The only two people in my life who I felt like genuinely cared for me, other than my sister, and I've lost them both. "I'd had a difficult night, and I ended up driving and showing up at the bar where he works. I didn't know who he was."

More tears stream down her face and she shakes her head like she knows what's coming. She's probably right and I don't know how to make the truth hurt any less, so I just say, "We slept together, neither one of us knew who the other was, but I still cheated on you, Amanda. I won't lie more and tell you it was a mistake, because it wasn't. I knew exactly what I was doing, and I wanted it. I wanted him. I wanted to know what it was like to be with a man. And he gave me that. When I called you the next morning it was after leaving his apartment. That was the night I proposed to you." I am crying now, silent tears sliding down my cheeks and her body is shaking, whether with rage or disgust or shock, or perhaps all three, I don't know. She steeples her hands over her mouth, her eyes closed.

"I never meant to hurt you, Amanda, but I know that's little consolation now."

There's a moment of silence before she says, her eyes still closed. "This whole time? You and him? You're the reason he left?"

"Yes," I say and she shakes her head again.

Neither one of us speaks again, but I leave the table and head upstairs. I'm back down only twenty minutes later with my suitcase packed haphazardly, and Amanda is gone. I head into the office and grab the things that are essential for work.

I've got my laptop, which will suffice for now, but I'll have to come back and pack up the larger things later.

I leave my key on the table and step outside.

Twenty minutes after that I'm knocking on my sister's door. How I even got here I don't know. I honestly was in no condition to be driving, and even though there's every chance in the world she's not even home, I have nowhere else to go.

I'm about to give up and wait for her in my car when the door opens and her face greets me. The minute I see her I burst into tears.

"Christ, Oliver, what on earth happened?" she says, taking me in her arms and hugging me tightly. I sob openly on her doorstep, not caring if the neighbors see or hear. I'm past that now. "Shhh," she soothes, "it'll be alright." But I'm terrified that after telling her what I've done she'll kick me out, too, and I wouldn't blame her if she did.

She coaxes me inside and shuts the door behind me. I leave my things in the entryway and she pulls me towards the living room. "Sit," she says, gently. "I'll make us some tea."

I sit and my body is shaking while I wait for her. I try to wipe away my tears, but more keep coming. She returns after a few minutes and hands me a cup, before sitting next to me.

"Freddie?" I ask.

"Napping," she tells me, with a small smile. "I'm sure he'll be glad to see you. He misses you."

I wipe more tears away and she hands me a tissue that I use to blow my nose. "Talk to me," she says.

"Christ, you'll fucking hate me," I say, shaking my head.

"Hey," she scolds gently, "if I was going to hate you it would be for the time you stole my Rapunzel barbie doll and then proceeded to cut off all of her hair because 'that's what happened in the movie'." She squeezes my arm and I can't help chuckling slightly, but then I'm sobbing some more.

"There's nothing you could ever tell me that will make me

hate you, Oliver. Nothing, do you understand? No matter how bad it is or how much you think you've messed up, I love you. I'm here for you. Whatever it is, I promise you're safe with me."

I look at her, her green eyes warm but concerned, and she wipes another tear from my cheek with her thumb.

"I...I slept with a man," I choke out. She blinks but doesn't gasp or scold me. Almost as if to make sure she understands, I add, "More than once."

"Why?" she simply says, and it's my turn to blink.

"What? Does it bloody matter? I fucking cheated on my fiancée, Olivia. And not even with some random guy. With her son."

Her eyes widen at this. "You what?"

"I fucked her son!" I almost shout before I remember that Freddie is napping down the hall.

"I'll have to admit I wasn't expecting that bit," she says, calm as ever.

My eyes narrow. "That bit?" I repeat. "You were expecting the rest of it?"

She bites her lip and nods. "I mean, maybe not those words, exactly, but..."

I swallow, my body shivering. "You knew?"

She shrugs. "I didn't know for certain but I thought it was quite probable. You never talked about liking girls, or having a crush on anyone growing up. Even when you took a girl to the school dances I could just tell you weren't enjoying your-self, but you did it to please Mother and Father, or to fit in with everyone else. I watched you shut down every single time they said anything homophobic, like it was personal. I can't imagine how that made you feel, Oli. Christ the things they said about queer people with you right there. I wanted to wring their necks, especially when I saw what it was doing to you. I wish I'd spoken up sooner than I did that night a few months ago. I hate myself for not, but I think it took me a while to find my voice."

I have tears streaming down my cheeks when she grips

my chin and turns me to face her. There's nothing but kindness and empathy when she speaks again, and I know I'm not worthy of it. I don't deserve grace or compassion right now. I wish she would yell at me, tell me what a horrible person I am and to get out of her house. It would be easier than this.

"I'm sorry you felt like you had to hide yourself for so long," she tells me. "I know being fed the bollocks like we were all those years must have made you feel like you had to do whatever it took to protect yourself, and I hate that for you. But you have a right to be who you really are, Oliver. You deserve to be happy with the person who makes you happy, no matter their gender or orientation. And I think that if you had felt like who you were was something to celebrate and take pride in, that you were good, and beautiful and worthy, instead of all the terrible things Mother and Father said, if you'd had the love and support you needed and deserved all these years you would have made much different choices. You should never have had to chase their love or approval."

I'm crying even more now but manage to choke out, "You either," and she gives a small smile.

"I'm realizing that, too," she says, moving her hand to mine and giving it a squeeze. "You are a good man. I'm not saying what you did was okay, and that there won't be consequences, but I understand why you felt so confused and why it would be difficult for you to accept that part of yourself after living with our parents. I'm honored that you told me." She chuckles. "Well, I'm assuming you're telling me you're gay, or bi, or pan, or something other than straight. I didn't actually let you share that part, did I? You don't have to, either. But if you want to tell me, I'm here, and I love you."

I squeeze her hand this time. Then I look at her. My voice is shaking and my hands are trembling. "I'm gay," I tell her, and she gives me the most beautiful smile. "God, Olivia, I'm as gay as the bloody rainbow."

She takes me in her arms as I sob, overwhelmed by it all;

by the fact that I just came out to my sister after twenty years; by the knowledge that my wedding isn't happening and I've lost my fiancée; by the years of built up hurt, grief and torment my parents caused, that I had tried to deny and ignore; and with the knowledge that I am very much in love with Hunter Price.

I've never been in love before, and I never expected it to hurt this much.

Fifteen

Three weeks later

HUNTER

I'm back at work now. And while I feel like I'm functioning better each day there are still moments where I find myself missing Oliver so much it hurts to breathe. I'm dreading returning home in a few weeks for the wedding, walking Mom down the aisle to the man I love, the man I've been trying to move on from.

The first several days of being back at my apartment after leaving Scarsdale were the worst. I was so upset I couldn't even bring myself to get out of bed the first three days. After that I didn't do anything other than mope around the apartment in my pajamas, eating way too much junk food and not even bothering to shower.

It took my roommates intervening for me to realize just how bad things had gotten, and I decided I needed to really get away, by myself, to just think and be and work though all of my feelings on my own. So I bought myself a ticket to Italy with the savings I'd acquired from work, even though financially it wasn't the wisest decision, I knew that for the sake of my mental and emotional wellbeing I had to do it.

I'd never been to another country before, and while it was frightening, being on my own and not speaking the language or knowing my way around, it also gave me something else to do, another way to occupy my mind, and I loved it. I visited Rome, Florence, Venice, and Milan, had the most delicious pasta and pizza I've ever tasted, and even took some cooking classes.

I took my time and did a lot of sightseeing. I visited the Colosseum, the Pantheon, and Trevi Fountain; toured the Catacombs, drank delicious wine, and went on a gondola ride on the Grand Canal.

I fell in love with the people and the country, and allowed myself to accept the fact that Oliver wasn't mine. That he wouldn't be mine, and didn't love me the way I loved him. And even though it was painful, and even though I cried as much as I smiled and laughed, my time in Italy healed me, restored me, revived me, and allowed me to begin to grieve the loss of the man I loved.

There was a part of me that would always love him, I knew that. But life was good and beautiful in itself, and that was something I needed to learn. That I could be happy without him. And that I couldn't make him love me back or force him to accept something he wasn't ready to accept, to be brave enough to choose himself and his own happiness, whether it was with me or not.

I would attend the wedding, and then it would be months before I saw Mom or Oliver again, and every visit would be short. Maybe they would even stop altogether. I didn't know.

I'd told him at the beginning that I knew what I was risking to be with him, that I accepted the consequences, and if I had it to do all over again, I wouldn't change a thing.

Because Oliver Jones was many things, but he was not regrettable.

OLIVER

I'm sitting with my nephew on my lap, reading him a story, when my phone buzzes. It's taking much longer than it should because he likes to point to all the pictures and have me tell him what they are, but I don't mind. I love his curiosity and the way he giggles or claps when he gets excited about something. And my heart melts when he calls me "Unca Owi." Being with him and my sister these past few weeks has been exactly what I needed. His smiles and hugs never fail to cheer me up, and I'm realizing just how happy Olivia is on her own, and how much she's thriving. It's given me the courage to make some pretty drastic changes in my own life, and while I'm terrified of upsetting the status quo I'm also rather excited about where I'm headed.

I pick up the phone and see that it's a text from Amanda, asking me if I can meet her for lunch the next day. To say I'm surprised is an understatement. I haven't seen or spoken to her since I left three weeks ago. I returned to the house to get the rest of my things but she said she would leave the spare key under the mat for me because she didn't want to see me. I understood, of course. I don't blame her one bit, but I'm surprised she's reaching out. I thought she'd never want to speak to me again.

Maybe she's ready to see me now and needs some closure. And I can give her that. It's the least I can do after what I put her through.

When I reply asking where and when, I get a text back with an address and a time, but nothing more.

"Tory, tory," Freddie chants, putting his chubby little hand on my cheek and raising the book. I set my phone back down and return my attention to him, pressing a kiss to his hair. Olivia is working today and I'm not, so I've got toddler duty, and that's all right with me. I'm planning to move out soon but I have some things I need to take care of first.

When I arrive at the restaurant the following afternoon I spot Amanda at a two person table and make my way over to her, somewhat cautiously, I must admit. She looks tired when I reach her but she offers me a small smile and gestures for me to sit.

"Hello," I say.

"Hi," she replies, then bites her lip. She's normally so confident, but she seems rather flustered now. "I'm guessing you were a little surprised to get my text?"

I nod.

"I uh…I just had some questions, if that's okay?"

I nod again. She reaches into her purse and pulls out the note. I'd forgotten it in my haste to leave, and she must have picked it up when she got back home. Though I'm surprised she didn't burn it or tear it apart and toss it in the waste bin. "This is yours," she says, and my eyes widen as she reaches across the table and places it in front of me. My gaze shifts from the note to her.

"I read it again," she says, stunning me even further. Tears fill her eyes and she wipes them away. "I was so focused the first time on the fact that my son was writing you a love letter, and I was so angry and hurt by the betrayal I felt, that I didn't read the other things he said. But I did this time. The way he talked like he knew a version of you I never did. Like you shared something with him, pieces of yourself I had never known. He talked like he knew the real Oliver. An Oliver that I didn't realize was hurting so much, struggling so much, because he believed that who he was wasn't worthy or love-able, and so he tried to be something else. And when that didn't work, he did something he never thought he would do. And I'm sorry, Oliver, that you felt like you had to put on a mask to make other people happy."

I shake my head. "You don't have anything to apologize for."

She wipes the tears from her cheeks and continues. "I'm not saying I forgive you. I don't know if that will happen any time soon, but I'm saying that you are a good person, and I recognize that, and so is my son, and even though I want to strangle you both, I don't want to hold on to anger or resentment, and I'm trying my best to understand the position you were in, how trapped you felt. I just wish you had said something sooner."

I shake my head again as tears fill my eyes. "You don't have to say that," I tell her. "I'm not a good person, and I don't deserve any of your understanding. I'm so sorry, Amanda, for not saying something sooner. For so many things."

"Well, you can thank your sister for the understanding," she tells me and my eyes widen.

"What?"

"She called me a while back to see how I was doing, said she had found out what happened. And when I got done telling her what an asshole her brother was, she asked if we could meet. When I agreed, she listened to me, and then asked if she could share a little bit about your household growing up. She did, and I realized that there were a lot of things about your parents I wasn't aware of, like how incredibly homophobic they are, and all the things they said to you both growing up. Things that would have made a gay teenager terrified of acknowledging his sexuality. I couldn't believe some of the things she told me. And I can't believe I never knew. I mean I know they're a bit controlling, but God, I didn't think they were pricks. Imagining Hunter growing up in that same environment, it made me sick."

I chuckle softly and feel a warmth spread through my chest at the knowledge that Olivia did that for me.

"The other thing that was made very clear to me in that letter, is how much Hunter loves you. And while I don't fully comprehend his actions, I don't want to be the cause of you two not being together if that's what you want. You deserve to be happy, Oliver. And if he makes you happy, then I want that for you."

"You're being far too kind, Amanda," I tell her.

"Probably," she agrees, "but I don't see the point in wishing hardship on people who've already had their fair share, and he's my son. There's nothing I wouldn't do for him."

"I believe you," I say, as another tear slides down her cheek.

"You love him, don't you?"

I nod, and my throat constricts. "Very much."

"Then go to him, Oliver," she tells me. "Make it right."

Two days later

"Wish me luck," I tell Olivia as I grab my keys and wallet. "I'm off to meet Mother and Father for dinner."

"Good luck," she says, fixing the collar of my dress shirt and then giving me a big hug. "I'm so proud of you."

"Thank you," I say, squeezing her back. I sigh. "They're not going to be happy."

"When are they ever?" she says, and I chuckle. "Do you want me to go with you? I could bring Freddie along or see if someone can watch him."

I shake my head. "No, I should go alone. This is something I need to do for myself. And I've decided to meet them in public so things hopefully will stay mostly civil."

She nods. "You know I support you. Be brave."

I give her one more hug before heading out the door.

When I enter the restaurant where I've asked Mother and Father to meet me, I tell the hostess who I'm with and she directs me to their table. They're sitting next to each other and I steel myself before sliding into the chair opposite them.

"Nice of you to join us, son," Father starts off. "We've been waiting here for fifteen minutes. Almost got up and left."

"What's going on, Oliver?" Mother pipes up. "You've been ignoring our calls and texts for weeks. Your sister told us the wedding was canceled but that can't be true."

"Yes, your mother was very upset by that news," Father says, scowling at me. "Surely Olivia was mistaken."

You're allowed to disappoint them. "She wasn't," I say. "The wedding is off. Amanda and I aren't getting married. I'm in love with someone else." Fuck, my heart is racing but I bloody did it.

Their eyes practically light up, no doubt assuming I'm referring to some woman a decade younger than me who will be utterly ecstatic about the idea of giving them grand-children.

"Well, don't keep us waiting, dear," Mother says. "Tell us about her."

I wiggle my toes, clenching and unclenching my fists on my lap, then take a deep breath. "Actually, it's a him."

They both stare at me, like they're sure they heard me wrong.

"I beg your pardon?" Mother says.

"He's joking, darling," Father says. "Our son isn't gay."

I grit my teeth. "Actually, Father, I am."

He balks. "Preposterous. Since when?"

"My entire bloody life, but you two were always too narrow minded to even consider the fact that you might have a queer child," I hiss.

"This is absurd," Father retorts, his voice a harsh whisper. "You are not gay, Oliver. You were engaged to a woman. I don't understand. You know better. Why would you choose to do this? To upset us like this?"

"Choose to upset you?" I say. "Being gay isn't a choice, Father, it's who I bloody am, and it took me until I was thirty-six to tell you because I knew you would respond this way."

"Respond in what way?" he asks, appalled.

"Make it about yourself," I tell him. "Tell me how wrong I am. Try to deny it."

"I don't know what you want, Oliver," Mother says, crying now.

"I want you to love me, for me," I tell her, almost shouting. This conversation has derailed rather quickly. "All my life I've done what you wanted me to do and been who you expected me to be. I've done everything I can to earn your love and it still wasn't enough. I got good grades. I went to the school you wanted me to go to. I got the bloody job you wanted me to get even though I fucking hated it. I dated who I knew you would want me to date. I lied to myself and everyone around me for years about who I was because you made me feel like being gay was the worst possible thing I could be; Like my existence offended you; Like I was less than human because of my sexuality. And I fucking believed you. But then I met a man who saw the real me and loved me for who I was, encouraged me to be me. Told me that I was worthy and good and that I deserved to be happy, even if it meant disappointing my parents. And even though he probably never wants to see me again after the way I treated him I am going to do my bloody best to get him back because he is what makes me happy."

"You're serious?" Father says as tears slide down my cheeks. "Well, that's ungratefulness for you. We've only ever wanted what was best for you, Oliver. I don't know why you can't see that. It's not right, a man being with another man."

"Christ," I mutter, wiping the tears away, and pulling my chair back to stand. "I don't have anything else to say. I'm going after Hunter. When you two get your heads out of your arses, let me know."

Mother's eyes widen and Father snarls.

"You're choosing that boy over us? Over your own family?"

"No, Father," I say, scooting my chair back in. "I'm

choosing me." Then I turn to walk away, but before I do I look back at them and say, "And by the way, I quit my job."

Sixteen

The next day

HUNTER

I'm behind the counter at work, wiping down a glass when I see a familiar reflection through the mirror on the wall in front of me. My heart stutters at the sight of him, and then his gaze meets mine.

"Hello, Hunter." I turn and take him in. He's wearing a button up shirt and shorts and he's gotten a nice tan since the last time I saw him. One that tells me he's been in the sun quite a bit, and not just during our trip. His hair is more wild than usual, and his eyes are bright, but wary, hands in his pockets.

"Hello, Oli," I reply. "Can I get you anything?" Fuck, I've missed him so much I want to jump over the counter and collide with him, touch him, taste him, feel him against me and make sure he's real. But I don't. Because I'm wary, too.

He steps closer to the counter. "I was hoping we could talk," he says, in a more hushed voice.

"I'm working," I reply, and start to walk away, even

though I have nowhere to go. There's one other person here right now and they've been taken care of.

"I quit my job," he blurts out, making me stop in my tracks and turn around. He's biting his lip and shuffling from foot to foot and it's so damn adorable that I can't stop my lips from quirking into a soft smile. He's running his fingers through his hair, eyes darting to the floor and then back to me. "I, uh, I just wanted you to know that."

"You came all the way here to tell me you quit your job?" I say, and he flushes. God, I love teasing him.

He clears his throat. "Well, not just to tell you that. I..." he looks around, and even though he seems nervous as hell it doesn't keep him from speaking. "I wanted to try and get you back."

"Does Mom know you're here?" I ask, frowning.

He nods. "She told me to find you."

I gape. "She what?"

"She knows, Hunter."

My heart thrashes. "You told her?"

He shakes his head. "She found your note."

Holy fuck. No wonder I haven't heard from her in a while. I talked with her the day after I got back to my apartment from Scarsdale but that was the last time. "Fuck, she must hate me," I say, running my fingers through my hair.

"She's upset and hurt, but I don't think she could ever hate you," Oliver tells me. "I think she needs time."

I nod. I never wanted to hurt her. And I'll always be sorry that my actions did hurt her, because I would never want to cause her pain, but I also know I can't apologize for being with Oliver. No matter how bad of a person that makes me. I don't know if that's something she'll ever be able to understand or forgive me for.

"You quit your job?" I ask, and he nods, a grin splitting his handsome face. God, I've missed that smile, my beautiful Oliver.

I scoot closer. "You said you wanted to try and get me

back?" My voice is lower and more sultry and his cheeks flush again. He nods.

"Shoot," I say.

"Fuck, you're going to make me work for this, aren't you?"

I grin, and it grows wider when he says, "I told my parents about you. I told them I'm gay."

"And?" I ask, when all I really want to do is leap over the counter and kiss him. Fuck, yeah, Oli.

"They didn't take it well." For some reason that makes me smile wider.

"And what did you tell them about me?" I ask.

He looks me straight in the eyes and says, "That I love you, Hunter Price. That I was going to do my bloody best to get you to forgive me because I can't imagine my life without you. That you are the best thing I've ever known. That you gave me the courage to be me, for the first time in my life, and to put myself first. That you taught me to love who I am."

Tears sting my eyes as my chest tightens. "You really said that?"

He nods. "Well, maybe not all those words exactly, but the general idea."

I can't help laughing, and then I'm moving out from behind the counter and going to him because I can't stand to be away from him for another second. I grip his face and kiss him so hard he stumbles back into the nearby stool, grunting as he lands on it, shrinking several inches in the process. I go with the flow, sliding between his thighs and tilting his head back to slip my tongue down his throat.

Fuck, I'm crazy for him.

"Did I do okay?" he asks once we part for air, and I laugh because he's so fucking cute. He flushes again, pressing his face to my abdomen.

"Yeah, Oli, you did okay," I tell him, lifting his chin to look at me. His eyes glisten with tears and I kiss him again. We part when we hear the one single patron clapping and whistling loudly.

Oliver's face flames but I just laugh again. "My break is due," I tell him. "Wanna reacquaint ourselves with the stockroom?"

He bites his lip and nods. I grab his hand and pull him up, and down the hall.

As soon as we're inside, I spin around and shove him up against the wall. "Need you," I say, my mouth claiming his and my hands gripping his wrists, holding them above his head. My leg slides between his thighs, spreading them, and he whimpers as my leg presses against his cock. He's rock hard already and I groan as he thrusts against me, whimpering incessantly.

"Fuck, Oli," I growl, pulling away. His gyrations don't stop and I grip his wrists harder, taking his chin into my other hand. "Fuck, you make me so damn hard." I kiss him again, rubbing my leg against his dick until he's a whimpering, whining mess. I move my hand from his chin to his hair and grip hard. His eyes flare and his thick cock jerks against my thigh.

"Tell me what you want, Oli," I say, my voice low and husky, then press kiss after kiss to the adorable freckles decorating his nose and cheeks, making him squirm.

I tug his hair harder, making his head tilt back, and he gasps. "I want you to fuck me," he says. "Hard." My cock jerks when he flushes and adds, "I want to be your good boy."

"Fuck, Oli." I kiss his lips again before making my way down his neck, biting and sucking, growling at the realization that I can fucking mark him wherever the hell I want now, because he's fucking mine. I don't waste any time, either. I suck and bite on his neck until he's shaking and whimpering, his breaths ragged and his cock twitching obscenely against my thigh. Then I'm moving my hand from his hair to fondle his cock and balls through his shorts. The moan that escapes him is fucking delicious. "So fucking pretty when you moan for me, Oli," I tell him, nuzzling his jaw with my nose. "You're gonna make so many pretty sounds when I'm fucking you, aren't you, baby?"

"Oh, God, Hunter, please," he whines, and I know he's close to tears. "Please I need you inside me. I'm so fucking hard. It's been so long."

I hum and press another kiss to his neck before undoing his belt and spinning him around. "Hands on the wall," I tell him, and he obeys eagerly. I slide my hand around and pop the button on his shorts, the small gasp he emits making my cock throb. God, he drives me wild. "I can't fucking wait to get inside you again," I growl as I slide his shorts and underwear down, letting them land around his ankles. His cock stands proud, so hard and desperate, the head red and angry already, precum sliding down his shaft. I slide my own pants and underwear down and then press up against him, both of us moaning at the feel of our naked skin against each other's again. He shoves his ass back and my cock jerks as if it knows exactly whose ass this is, and can't wait to get inside where it belongs.

"Fuck, Oli." I reach one arm around and place my palm on his abdomen, holding him to me, then slide the other hand around and grip his cock, feeling the familiar weight of it in my palm and moaning at the sensation. "God, I've missed this cock," I tell him, stroking it languidly.

"Ngggg," he whimpers, squirming as I run my hand from his abdomen up his pecs where I rub my finger over his hardening nipples. I stay there for a moment, his cock jerking like crazy in my hand as I continue to stroke him slowly. "Beg me, Oli," I whisper in his ear, sliding my hand from his cock and bringing it back to his ass where I run it down his crack, stopping at his hole. I press my finger against it and he whimpers. "Beg me to fuck this pretty hole."

"Please," he cries. "Please, Hunter, I need you. Please fuck me. Please." His hole flutters against my finger and I press it inside him, hearing him mewl as I slide deeper, his ass clenching around my finger, slick with his precum.

"Oh, God," he whines. "Yes, more. Please, more. I need more."

"Fuck, baby, you're gonna make me fucking come before I even get inside you if you keep talking like that," I warn him.

He whimpers again, and I can't fucking wait anymore. "Can I take you bare?" I ask.

He nods quickly. "Yes, Christ, yes, I'm negative."

My cock throbs at that and I kiss his neck. "Me, too," I tell him, before reaching down to grab a packet of lube from my wallet. I slick myself up and then line my cock up with his hole. Gripping his hair in one hand and his hip with the other, I press inside him, and holy fucking hell, it's so much more intense than I even imagined. "Shit, Oli," I moan as I press in slowly, the heat and suction so fucking incredible that I have to slide out some before pushing back in or I'll come before I'm even fully sheathed. I let out a deep breath as he swallows me inch by inch. "Goddamn, baby, you feel so fucking incredible. So fucking good, Oli."

I slide my hand along his back, moaning like a fucking whore as I bottom out. Then I'm resting my head against his upper back, taking in another deep breath as I hold him to me. I can feel him shaking against me, his ass clenching and unclenching around my cock. I tighten my grip on his hair and he whimpers, his ass tightening around me at the same time. "I'm so fucking hard, baby," I tell him. "God, this is not going to last long. I'm gonna take you hard and fast, and we're gonna come together, okay, beautiful? I want you too much right now for anything else."

He nods and I dig my fingers into his hip and slide out part way before pushing back in, hard. "Fuck," he cries, as I slam into him again and again, my cock nudging his prostate each and every time.

"Fuck, baby," I moan, my grip on him tightening. "Fuck, you're perfect, Oli. So damn perfect. Love this ass, sweetheart.

Gonna fill you up so good, baby." I move my hand from his hip to his cock and stroke him in tandem with my thrusts.

"Oh, God," he wails. "So good, Hunter. So bloody good."

"Come for me, baby," I tell him. I slam into him two more times and yank on his hair, tilting his head back as we both shout out our releases, his cock pulsing in my grip and spraying all over the wall and my hand as I bite down on his neck, my own release spilling inside him.

"Fuck." His chest rises and falls as he supports himself on the wall, trembling with the aftershocks of his release.

"So good for me, Oli," I say, pressing kisses to his back through his shirt and nuzzling his neck. "So perfect for me. My good boy."

Epilogue

5 years later

HUNTER

I smile as I sip on my coffee and watch my husband through the large floor to ceiling windows of our home just outside of Scarsdale. We lived in a smaller place until recently when Oliver's income started growing again. He'd taken a bit of a pay cut after quitting his accounting job, but the payoff of seeing him so happy was more than worth it.

He's shirtless, wearing a simple pair of jeans, kneeling in the soil of the flower garden he designed right after we purchased this house.

I feel a wet tongue against my fingers and look down at the brown ball of fur by my side, tongue out and tail wagging as he stares out the window at Oliver, too.

"He'll be inside soon, boy," I tell him, then scratch behind his ear, making him tilt his head and thump his foot against the floor. Clifford is the cavapoo we adopted a little over a year ago and he adores Oliver, though he's fond of me as well. He's sweet, exuberant, playful, and a wonderful addition to our family. Oliver picked him out after I told him I wanted to get him a dog as a birthday present. I told him he could have any one he wanted and when we got to the animal shelter this little furball stole his heart in an instant. Apparently his previous owner had only had him for a short while before finding out their child was severely allergic, and their loss was our gain.

Oliver and Clifford instantly bonded, and they've been almost inseparable ever since, the canine following him around every moment of the day when Oliver is home and lying just inside the front door when he isn't.

Even now, Clifford moves to the door and begins to paw at it, whimpering, and I give up and open it, letting him free. He rushes around the house and the next thing I see through the window is Clifford bounding headlong towards my husband and Oliver tumbling backwards as the dog slobbers all over his face, him laughing hysterically. I smile at the duo and sip my coffee as Oliver's dirty hands reach up and grip Clifford's face, trying to distance himself from the onslaught.

After quitting his accounting job five years ago, Oliver went to work for a landscaping company and was able to learn enough on the job and with a few night classes that he opened his own landscaping business about a year ago, and now has around a dozen people that he employs, and has done all of the design for our two story suburban home. He thrives at his job, and I have never seen him more happy than when he's working outside, soaking up the sun and fresh air, surrounded by nature. And I'll never complain about seeing him on his knees.

I've been working on finishing up my doctorate in child psychology, and it's been exhausting, but rewarding, and I have never regretted my decision for a second, especially when Oliver looks at me with so much pride and fondness, and I know he hasn't stopped bragging about me to his friends and employees.

I watch as he wipes the sweat from his brow with his forearm, having finally managed to extract himself from the dog who now stands beside him, panting and wagging his tail. The sunlight bounces off Oliver's gold wedding band, making it sparkle. He turns and spies me staring at him through the window and gives me that tell tale Oliver flush and smile that has butterflies taking flight in my stomach. I can't get enough of this man, and seeing him come into himself, seeing him take charge of his own life, living the life he deserves, for himself, has been my greatest privilege.

We got married 3 years ago, and all of our friends were there, my old roommates from college came, the friends and coworkers that Oliver met on the job, Olivia, and Freddie, who we asked to be our flower boy and who consequently stole the show, and even Mom and her boyfriend, Mark.

Things are better between us. It's taken time, but we talked eventually. I had texted her to see if she wanted to talk shortly after Oliver and I got back together. She told me she loved me, but that she needed time, and that honestly she didn't think she could handle a conversation yet, or even hearing my voice. And of course I didn't blame her. I knew there was a chance she might never speak to me again after what I had done to her, how I'd hurt and betrayed her, and she had every right to walk away from me completely. She said she was going to go on her honeymoon alone and she would contact me when she felt ready.

It was a year later when she finally did call, and only a couple of weeks after we'd gotten engaged, and when I heard her voice I immediately started crying. I honestly wasn't sure if I would hear from her after everything. I told her I understood if she never wanted to speak to me again and if this call was just for closure and a way to say goodbye, it was more than I deserved, and the least that I owed. She told me she was not okay with the way I had treated her, but that she would like to start rebuilding our relationship if that was something I wanted, and we've slowly but surely been reconnecting. She said she'd forgiven me for the part I played in hurting her, and that she wanted me to be happy. She also told me she'd met someone, but that they were taking things slow. I told her about the wedding and said I understood if she didn't want to come, but that it was several months away so she had time to think about it, and while I certainly didn't expect her to come, I would love it if she did. I told her I would leave it up to her to make contact in the future, always willing to take things at her pace, and if she ever changed her mind and decided she couldn't be a part of my life, I would grieve, but I would understand.

We agreed to meet up a couple of times a month in the months leading up to the wedding, and while things were awkward, especially at first, I was just glad she wanted to be in my life again. I don't know if things between us will ever be the way they were before, but we're trying, and I am grateful, because I do love her.

When she did show up at the wedding I was stunned. I sobbed when she hugged me and said, "You might have been okay with losing me, Hunter, but I am not okay with losing you. You're my son." I know that I'll never understand the grief and pain and anger she dealt with, the heartache, the amount of work she must have done to get to where she was then, and where she is now. I know I don't deserve any of her kindness. Having her at our wedding meant everything to me.

We honeymooned in Europe, and Oliver was more than happy to be my guide in England, while I took over in Italy. Seeing the area where he grew up and the country he loved so much was such a beautiful experience, as was taking him to all the places I'd visited on my "get over Oliver" trip. Everything was infinitely better the second time around, with him as my husband.

I grab a glass of iced tea and bring it out to him, and he stands and wipes the dirt from his jeans before smiling and taking it, guzzling it down, sweat clinging to his ivory skin as Clifford worms his way between our legs, staring up at us both with those big brown eyes.

"Almost done?" I ask.

He nods.

"I'll make us some lunch then," I say, taking the glass and heading back inside, but not before patting Clifford on the head.

I pull out the bread, lettuce, tomato, mayo, and bacon, and make us sandwiches. Oliver loves BLTs.

When he gets inside, he showers and then joins me in the kitchen, pressing a kiss to my cheek, Clifford at his feet.

"Thank you," he says. "This looks amazing."

That afternoon we do a few more chores around the house and then after dinner we take Clifford on a walk, before he cuddles up next to me on the sofa and we listen as Oliver plays the piano. We got it a couple of years ago after he decided he wanted to take it up again, and watching and listening to him play is the highlight of my evenings.

He plays for himself, because he wants to. Because he loves it, and not out of a sense of obligation or the act of a child trying to earn the love of their parents, and it shows. He's incredibly talented, and I find it so relaxing.

His parents never did come around to the idea of their son being gay, and they haven't spoken to him since he told them about us. But it's their loss, and neither of us have any desire to change things. Of course he would rather they be accepting, but we're happy, and we have plenty of family and friends by our side. Olivia has also cut ties with her parents in support of Oliver, and because she says the only reason she stuck around in the first place after they shamed her for her divorce, was to support her brother.

We make love that night, and as I move inside my husband, my arms around him, holding him close as he clings to me, letting out the most beautiful sounds, our sweat slicked bodies entangled, I can't imagine anywhere else I would rather be than here with this incredible man, who's made my life infinitely better just by being him. I'm so incredibly proud of him, for having the courage to face his fears and accept himself for the beautiful person that he is.

Marrying him was an honor, and growing old with him is a privilege. I can't wait to see where life takes us, because with him by my side I know I'll always be home.

I hear his cry of pleasure as he releases between us and I come inside him, then press kisses to his sweat slicked skin and breathe in the scent of gingerbread and vanilla.

The scent of Oliver.

The End

Thank you so much for reading Oliver and Hunter's story. If you enjoyed it please consider leaving a review!

Want More?

Wondering if Hunter ever followed through on his promise to make Oliver come just from praising him? Find out by signing up for my newsletter. It gets sent out on the first of every month and all of my short stories are included in each edition.

https://felicitysnow.substack.com

Can't wait? You can also purchase it for $0.99 from my payhip website here: https://payhip.com/b/ORoca

About the Author

I live in sunny Florida with my husband and three children. I love reading and writing mm romance and am an advocate of mental health and chronic pain awareness. I love rainy days and sunshine and curling up with a good book or watching my favorite tv shows. I'm a big fan of the tv show Supernatural and believe that Starbucks is a form of self-care :)

You can follow me on social media, join my facebook group Felicity Snow's Followers, sign up for my newsletter, see my Pinterest storyboards, and find my other books here:

https://linktr.ee/felsnowauthor